COMPLICITY IN HEEL$

A MONEY LAUNDERERS' TALE

Publisher's Cataloging-In-Publication Data
(Prepared by The Donohue Group, Inc.)

Names: Leatherwood, Matt.
Title: Complicity in heels : a money launderers' tale / Matt Leatherwood Jr.
Description: 1st ed. | Augusta, Georgia : Epic Spin Publishing, [2016] | Series:
    [The Nikki Frank collection] ; [1]
Identifiers: ISBN 978-0-9883986-1-0 | ISBN 978-0-9883986-0-3 (ebook)
Subjects: LCSH: Women ex-convicts—United States—Fiction. | Money
    laundering—United States—Fiction. | United States—Officials and
    employees—Fiction. | United States—Economic conditions—Fiction. |
    Brothers and sisters—Fiction. | LCGFT: Thrillers (Fiction)
Classification: LCC PS3612.E2397 C66 2016 (print) | LCC PS3612.E2397
    (ebook) | DDC 813/.6—dc23

Epic Spin Publishing
400 West Peachtree Street NW
Suite #4-751
Atlanta, GA 30308

www.mattleatherwoodbooks.com

Printed in the United States of America

Publisher's note: This is a work of fiction. Names, characters, places, and
incidents are products of the author's imagination. Locales and public names are
sometimes used for atmospheric purposes. Any resemblance to actual people,
living or dead, or to businesses, companies, events, institutions, or locales is
completely coincidental.

Cover design by Damonza.com

Complicity in Heels: A Money Launderers' Tale/Matt Leatherwood Jr. — 1st ed.
ISBN 978-0-9883986-1-0

"If you live among wolves, you have to act like a wolf."

—Nikita Khrushchev

Barbara Jean Leatherwood
(October 24, 1939—February 17, 2006)

"Finished!"

ACKNOWLEDGMENTS

THANK YOU TO the following individuals. Without their contributions and support, I couldn't have written and published this book.

Michael Crawley, my instructor at Winghill Writing School. Thank you for teaching me the craft of fiction writing.

Larry Brooks, author and story coach (www.storyfix.com). Thank you for your expert analysis of this story's concept, your positive affirmation, and the title suggestion.

Angela Brown, my seasoned editor. Thank you so much for your assistance in refining this story. Your keen eye, industry expertise, and command over language helped me further develop as a writer. I'm so pleased with the final product and truly believe we have an audience winner.

COMPLICITY IN HEEL$

A MONEY LAUNDERERS' TALE

MATT LEATHERWOOD JR.

CHAPTER ONE

Owen County; Twenty Miles Outside of Parkbridge, Georgia

The automated gates to the Madelyn P. Shaw Women's Correctional Facility clanked shut. Inmate #30822 stepped forward as the white Chrysler 300C limousine pulled up to the curb. The chauffeur placed the luxury vehicle in park, stepped out from behind the steering wheel, and made his way toward the passenger side.

The well-groomed man, wearing a clean, crisp suit with a matching chauffeur cap, opened the door. "Ms. Frank," he said, motioning with his free arm for her to get into the 300C.

Nikki hesitated. *What in the world?*

"Ms. Frank, please," he prompted again. The repetitive sound of the engine droned on in the background.

"All right, Paris Oaks Assisted Living Facility then."

Nikki ducked her head and climbed inside the vehicle. The interior was trimmed in a Circassian walnut veneer that complemented the limo's sandstone leather seats. A minibar contained an assortment of alcoholic beverages along with Italian-cut champagne flutes and etched glassware. On the seat near the partition sat Spencer Taylor, holding a glass of Martell Cordon Bleu. He was a peach-skinned man, six foot one, with brass-blond hair. His stubbly beard contained more brown strands of hair than blond, giving his square face a dull appearance. Spence took a quick sip of the cognac then placed the glass back on top of the minibar. "Long time no see."

Nikki stared at the three gift boxes next to her on the seat. "Three years, six months, and nine days, but who's counting?"

"Apparently you are. I thought it was a five-year sentence."

"It was. I got a year off for good behavior, and with the overcrowding situation, my being a nonviolent offender pushed my release date up even sooner."

"Fantastic. It's great to see you again, Nikki."

"I'd say the same thing, but my last memory was of you shoving me to the ground and hightailing it in the opposite direction to avoid arrest."

A smug look swept across Spence's face.

The chauffeur eased the limo into traffic. An awkward moment of silence passed. Nikki took a deep breath. Jasmine and bergamot from Spence's cologne filled the cabin. The smell was refined, refreshing.

She motioned to the gifts beside her. "All this," she said, changing topics, "seems a bit over the top, don't you think?"

"Over the top?" He shook his head. "Not for my girl. You deserve the best. Don't think I don't appreciate you doing the time."

"Frequent visits would've sufficed…or at least one visit."

Spence simply nodded.

"A letter, phone call, something," Nikki added. "As they say, actions speak a lot louder than words."

He sighed. "Look, it wasn't my call. Shortly after your arrest, Cordoza had us disband and go underground for nine months. We worked as much as we could independently. We just didn't associate publicly. We were secretive about meetings and communication. When we finally did resurface, an entire year had passed since your arrest. Don't you think I wanted to visit you?

Write you a letter? Make a phone call? Panic set in—everyone was scared. We didn't know if you were gonna toe the line or crack under pressure. Either way, we had to assume the authorities had you under surveillance while you were in prison."

"You guys overreacted."

Spence let out a huff. "No, we didn't. That's your ego talking."

The comment surprised Nikki. Spence was right; she just didn't want to hear it. Switching topics again, she asked about his suit.

Spence grinned. "Custom designed by our friend Big Al on Lennox and Fifth. Single-breasted jacket, black with white-wine pin-stripes. Matching vest and wide-legged trousers. Gorgeous, huh?"

Nikki nodded. "Impressive. Looks like you've done well since I've been gone."

"Don't worry. I picked something up for you as well." He motioned to the packages next to her.

Nikki grabbed the largest box first and opened it: a Vera Wang maize-colored cocktail dress.

"Dupioni silk. Big Al had it shipped in last night, express from New York."

Nikki's fingers ran over the shimmering fabric. It felt so good to the touch, so much more elegant than the prison uniform she'd worn the past few years. Without hesitation, she removed her thrift-store-issued, peony-print blouse, exposing a standard white bra beneath. The contours of her breasts jutted forward.

Spence's greenish-blue eyes widened. "What are you doing?"

Ignoring him, she removed her pants. Spence caught a glimpse of her skin, with its nutmeg and reddish undertone, that had been concealed beneath the denim. Nikki's seminude body revealed the sleek muscle tone and definition from her consistent workouts in the prison yard.

Spence quickly hit the partition switch to activate the tinted glass privacy divider. "Are you nuts?"

"Look," Nikki said, "I've been showering with thirty to sixty women every night for the last three-plus years, so whatever shred of modesty I might've once had is long gone. The last thing I'm worried about is you or the driver ogling me while I change."

Spence gawked in disbelief.

"Besides," Nikki said, easing the straps of the dress over her shoulders, "I gained the unwanted attention of the warden and found myself on some of his 'special hygiene' details."

Spence frowned.

"He'd often say, 'Hygiene inspections are a necessary formality in the running of an efficient penal facility,' then smirk. Funny thing was, there were never any medical staff present at any of the routine checkups."

"That's foul."

Nikki raised the dress's side zipper up. "Maybe, but it is what it is."

Spence shook his head.

The designer dress accentuated the symmetrical curves of Nikki's athletic frame. "Nice fit," she said. "Glad to see you got the size right."

Spence picked his glass up again and took a drink, then another one. "Of course I got it right."

"As well you should."

"Handpicked the dress myself."

Nikki gathered her secondhand clothing together. She reached into her pants pocket and removed a folded white envelope. Inside was a fourteen-karat-gold dog-tag pendant necklace along with a twenty-dollar bill.

She discarded the envelope, stuffed the cash down her bra, and held on to the pendant. "Burn these," she said, gesturing to her clothes on the seat.

"Absolutely."

Nikki stared at the pendant. Etched on the highly polished surface was an image of her marine father and toddler self. She turned the pendant around and read the inscription: "So small, so sweet, so loved. —Dad.'"

"What's that?" Spence asked.

Nikki put the necklace on. "Nothing."

"If you say so."

She grabbed the second box, held it for a moment to admire the silver wrapping paper, then opened it up: Jimmy Choo matching heels. Nikki smiled. Handmade. *Not bad*, she thought. *Not bad at all.*

"So…" Spence said, placing his glass back on the minibar. "They meet with your approval?"

"Yes. Definitely a yes." Excited, Nikki ran her fingers across the intricate suede-and-Chantilly-lace trim before trying them on. "These are amazing."

"I'm glad you like them."

She finished sliding into the heels—which, like the dress, fit perfectly—then looked up from the floorboard. Their eyes locked. Spence was drawn into the golden-brown starburst of her pupils, which bled into several yellow-and-blue streaks, making her eyes look green.

Nikki reached over and opened the final box. Inside was a makeup kit, hairbrush, and compact. She recognized the brand instantly, Cover Girl Queen Collection. Her face melted into an expression of sheer joy. With limited access to hair and beauty products on the inside, Nikki had found herself, like so many female prisoners before her, using food, lotion, and other facility items to concoct her own makeup. "Fakeup" they called it. She opened the compact and looked in the mirror. The prison-aged image reflected back to her was four years older and showed laugh lines around the mouth and hair that was beginning to thin. *Haggard*, she thought. *I'm just thirty. Where's my youth gone?* She adjusted her head in a couple of different angles then applied her makeup.

Spence folded his arms across his chest and tensed up his body. "Now let's talk business."

"So soon?" Nikki said, putting the makeup away. "You sure know how to kill a mood."

Business was the last thing she wanted to talk about. Thoughts of a warm bubble bath, a nice filet mignon with a glass of red wine, and a visit with brother, Marty, preoccupied her mind. Nikki continued to stare past Spence, creating an illusion of undivided attention.

Spence ignored the snide remark. "We've come a long way since you've been gone. No more ATM boosts, check-cashing scams, electronic pickpocketing, or identity theft. We've gone corporate, so to speak."

"Corporate?"

"Corporate," he repeated proudly. "What do drug dealers, organized crime outfits, and anyone else on the take, generating large amounts of cash, need?"

"One helluva defense attorney."

Spence laughed. "Besides that?"

Nikki shrugged. *I'm in no mood to play games*, she thought.

For a few seconds, the two of them sat quietly.

Spence broke the silence. "Someone to make ill-gotten gains appear legitimate."

"Money laundering?"

"Bravo. Or street magic, as I like to call it."

Nikki took a deep breath while she processed what she'd just heard. Instinctively she knew Spence was onto something. Laundering money would better insulate the crew from the violence of the street, expose them to a greater network of criminals, and had the potential to increase their profit margin severalfold, globally. And the best part? The client always supplied the product while the crew determined the means.

"Well, Houdini, seems like you've got it all figured out. What do you need me for?" she asked blithely, although she definitely was curious about her role.

Spence chuckled. "Nice to see prison hasn't robbed you of your quaint sense of humor."

"No, just my modesty, my sense of style, and the length of my hair."

"Cordoza's done a lot, and we've done two deals so far…small, less than a hundred thousand each," he explained. "But to take this to the next level—where we should be—we need another outside-the-box thinker besides me. Your idea to use Bluetooth technology to skim ATMs for cash was one of my all-time favorite schemes. Who would have thought short-range wireless communication could be so easily manipulated to generate a five-figure income?"

Nikki grinned, acknowledging Spence's praise. It was quite easy: attach a skimming device to an ATM, mount a false key-pad, then use Bluetooth to transmit the card number and PIN to a remote laptop in real time. If the process were executed properly, a single afternoon could net 2,500 card numbers and PINs with relative ease.

"Anyway, to level the playing field with, larger, more experienced money-brokering groups, I've been working on a program that takes advantage of the nation's ACH Network."

Nikki recognized the acronym for the Automated Clearing House, a national electronic network for financial transactions that processed large volumes of credit and debit-card transactions in batches. Last year alone, the network had been used to pay $9.2 billion in consumer bills nationwide: everything from cable-TV bills to home mortgages. "ACH," Nikki repeated, suddenly realizing the implications. "This could be huge."

"That's the idea." Spence's eyes crinkled at the edges as he smiled, exposing his perfectly straight teeth.

"If you could pull this off, you wouldn't just level the playing field, you'd severely tilt it in your favor."

Spence lowered the tinted glass divider to get some air circulating within the cabin. "Tilt it? Obliterate is more like it. However..." He hesitated.

"However what?"

"I've encountered some resistance on two fronts. For one, the source code has turned out to be more difficult than anticipated, putting me behind schedule. That's where you come in. With both of us attacking this 'project' from separate angles, not only will we get back on track, but we could possibly exceed expectations."

"And the second?" Nikki asked.

"Lacey Johnson."

Nikki leaned forward. "Lacey who?"

"Cordoza's latest stiletto-heeled vixen," Spence replied, casting a sour look. "Took up shop with us shortly after your arrest. Been with us ever since. She's got the boss man skipping to her beat, and the only way to keep him focused is to keep them separated. It's like he's got ADD or something."

Nikki wondered if Cordoza's penchant for strip clubs had finally gotten the better of him, his past having been a revolving door of buxom blondes, mysterious brunettes, and redheads with far too much attitude for their own good.

"Can't wait to meet her," she lied. On the one hand, Nikki was curious about this new woman who had asserted so much influence over Cordoza; on the other, she didn't want to deal with the drama Lacey would inevitably bring forth. Three and a half years at the women's correctional facility had provided more than enough drama for her in this lifetime.

For instance, there was Adamant Ann, a prison activist protesting everything from strip searches to religious rights, who'd filed so many grievances within a five-year period that the warden had hired a special mediator just to deal with her complaints on a day-to-day basis. And who could forget Malady Molly? She'd spent more time in the infirmary than on her prison work detail.

There wasn't an ailment out there that she wasn't familiar with or supposedly had at one time or another—from the common flu to food poisoning to obscure tropical diseases. And finally Brawling Betty: an aggressive inmate who thrived on physical confrontation. Her rage made no distinction between corrections staff or inmates, ultimately leading to her doing half her time in the hole, separated from general population. Drama was something Nikki was well versed in but had no desire to deal with now that she was out of prison.

"Oh, you'll get your chance," Spence warned her, glancing at the Cartier on his wrist. "In about ten minutes, when we pull into the Compound."

Nikki realized the limousine had gradually diverted from her original destination to an area that she'd once been familiar with but now barely recognized.

Dominion East, a rundown corridor in downtown Parkbridge, had been revived with an overabundance of commercial establishments. Dilapidated buildings had given way to new affordable housing, while parking garages and sidewalks had seemingly sprouted up overnight to support the increase in consumer foot traffic. Gone were the properties with for sale signs, vacant burned-out structures, and other decrepit sites. The steady flow of redevelopment dollars, along with the local government's judicious use of eminent domain, had transformed the economically depressed area into a thriving Mecca.

Nikki felt strange; so much had changed since she'd been gone. Adjusting would be awkward, maybe even difficult.

"Excuse me," she said, in an effort to gain the driver's attention. "Didn't I say Paris Oaks?"

"Yes, Ms. Frank, you did. But…" The chauffeur adjusted the rearview mirror to avoid eye contact with her.

Nikki tilted her head to the side to compensate. "But what? You're not familiar with the city?"

He shook his head. "No, I can assure you—"

"Willard is doing exactly what I asked him to do," Spence said, activating the partition switch once again for privacy.

The limo turned onto North Hill, sped past two yellow lights, then merged with traffic on Columbia Heights.

"Look," Nikki said, directing her attention back to Spence. "Drop me off at Paris Oaks, like I asked."

Spence's mouth broke into a devilish smirk. "In due time."

The 300C slowed to a crawl as it approached a gated driveway that Nikki recognized as the entrance to the Compound. Disappointed, she shook her head. A sensor on the gate detected the vehicle's presence and alerted the groundskeeper, who flipped a switch to give the limo free passage.

"This isn't funny, Spence. It's been three and a half years, and I'd really like to go see my brother. Sooner rather than later."

"Hey, we're all family here. Besides, the crew's inside." Spence made a welcoming gesture with his hands. "They're anxious to see you. Wouldn't it be rude not to stop by on the day of your release and say hi?"

Nikki was incredulous. "What? You've gotta be kidding me. Where was all this goodwill when I was up at Shaw? Funny how we're family when it's convenient for you."

The limo picked up speed for about hundred yards then came to a stop. "We're here," Willard announced.

"Please, just fifteen minutes, Nikki. That's all I'm asking. Then I'll have Willard drop you off at Paris Oaks to visit Marty."

Nikki grabbed hold of her thrift-store clothing. "Fifteen minutes, not a second more."

Spence smiled.

"Damn you!" she said, hurling them in his direction.

The abrupt reaction caught Spence off guard. He gathered the clothes and set them aside. "Nikki, Nikki, Nikki, always the consummate professional."

Willard opened the passenger door, breaking up the scene. "Ms. Frank," he called out, extending his arm to help her out of the limo.

Nikki grabbed his hand and moved to exit the vehicle. "Well, Spence, from one professional to another, don't think this makes us even. It'll take more than a limo ride and gifts to make restitution." *A lot more*, she thought.

Spence didn't reply. Nikki grinned as she exited the Chrysler.

CHAPTER TWO

Victor Patrone sat in a corner booth at the Urban Spoon Diner. He was a rakish man, with a long, clean-shaven face and tar-black hair swept down over his forehead. His back to the wall, he scanned the room for possible threats. Two came to mind: the heavyset guy leaning on the counter and the young man with a high and tight coming out of the restroom. Both caught his attention for different reasons. The considerable size of the guy at the counter made him a poor choice to engage in a physical altercation with, and the buzz cut on the young one clearly marked him as military. Who knew what kind of special skill set he possessed? If something went down, he calculated, the best weapons of choice would be the glass ketchup bottle in front of him or the steak knife on the dirty plate a table over. Victor preferred not to use the Beretta 9mm concealed beneath his Canali suit jacket if he didn't have to. It was an option of last resort, especially in a public place. With all this in mind, he completed his scan. The remaining patrons, as far as he could tell, posed no danger. Their empty hands and blank faces, mixed with the monotonous drone of idle conversation, further confirmed that no one was out to get him.

Victor's afternoon appointment was running late. Ten minutes already had passed, during which time he'd assessed the room, placed an order, and taken a leak. The diner was packed with its lunchtime crowd. The fifties decor, with its red-and-white checkerboard floor and vintage jukebox, provided an ambience of an era long past.

"Grilled portabella mushroom on wheat?" the waitress asked, confirming Victor's order.

"Yes," he replied.

She placed the food on the table and handed him some napkins. "All right then, here you go."

He paused for a moment to read her name tag: Jennifer.

"Thank you, Jennifer."

"My pleasure. If you need anything else, be sure to let me know." The twenty-something waitress handed Victor his bill and moved on to the next table.

Victor kept his eyes on her rear end. *Great ass*, he thought. *Definitely worth exploring.* A smile spread across his face, vivid carnal acts already having transpired in his head.

Just off to the side, a middle-aged man with ash-brown hair and a Chevron mustache stood watching. His off-the-rack, navy-blue suit was somewhat too big for his wiry frame. "She's young enough to be your daughter," he said, interrupting Victor's train of thought. "Or mine for that matter. Put your tongue back in your mouth, and let's get down to business."

Victor turned his head to the left. "Have a seat, Bosky."

"*Lieutenant* Bosky," he corrected, before sliding into the booth.

"That's right. The precinct recently promoted you based on performance," Victor mocked. "You should be a little more cordial. After all, if it weren't for the inside information I've been providing, your stellar performance wouldn't be so stellar."

A disdainful look etched across Bosky's oval face, making his curved chin appear pointed. "Let's not pretend you're doing me any favors, Patrone. Everybody involved knows this is quid pro quo work. The Lascano cartel sets aside ten to fifteen percent of product just for confiscation, then tips us off about shipments in the local area. The other eighty-five to ninety percent flies under the radar to meet street demand, and we still look good in the eye of the general public. Win-win."

Victor smirked. "It's a dirty game. Be careful who you mess with and who you don't."

Bosky held out his hand. "You have something for me?"

Victor took a bite of his sandwich. The roasted peppers and pesto sent a tidal wave of flavor throughout his mouth. "First things first."

"All right, I'm listening." The police officer propped his elbows up on the table and steepled his fingers.

"Well, as you know, quarterly collections are coming up. Quinn wants you to ensure that your patrol officers focus most of their attention on the Southside Locos and away from us. Our street-level crews need the harassment-free time."

Bosky raised an eyebrow. "Southside Locos, huh?"

Victor took another bite of his sandwich. "That's right. Might as well knock out the main competition while we're at it, wouldn't you agree?"

"A dealer is a dealer, regardless of crew, as long as I get paid," Bosky said with a shrug.

Victor put down his sandwich, removed a prepaid Visa card from inside his jacket, then slid it across the table toward the officer. "Would it have killed you to have that suit tailored properly?"

Bosky grabbed the card and examined it. "What's this?"

"Payment, twenty-first-century style," Victor replied. "Large white envelopes stuffed with cash are a relic of the past."

"Well, I'm a traditionalist," Bosky stated in a tone of sarcasm.

Victor picked up his sandwich again. "Go ahead. Call the eight-hundred number on the back."

Bosky pulled out his cell phone and dialed the number. An

automated teller answered the call. "Please enter the sixteen digit number that appears on the front of your prepaid card." He punched in the sequence of numbers. "Your available balance is eight thousand dollars and zero cents."

Bosky hung up the phone. "What's going on here, Patrone?" Victor looked up from his sandwich. "The fee Quinn and I negotiated," the lieutenant continued, "was ten thousand. By my count, you're two grand short."

Victor's blank expression revealed little. "About that...well, seems like there's been a restructuring of the payroll system."

Bosky's eyes narrowed. "Restructuring?"

"Yes," Victor said, leaning back into the booth and wiping his mouth with a napkin. "From now on, twenty percent of all your proceeds belong to me."

Bosky laughed. "You can't be serious."

"Dead serious."

"We'll see," Bosky protested. "Wait till I get a hold of Quinn and let him know the side action you're trying to muscle for yourself. My daughter's tuition is due at the end of the month, and you're pissing away my time with games."

"Daughter? Weren't you mumbling something about daughters a few moments ago when you walked in?"

Bosky stood. "Yeah, so?"

"If I recall, you expressed disapproval over my leering at the hot, young waitress over there behind the counter."

"That's right."

Victor could tell Bosky was getting frustrated. Most cops loved to conduct interrogations, but relatively few wanted to sit through one. "In my opinion, that whole incident was just a grandiose display of a paternal instinct to protect."

"Clearly something you know nothing about. Get to the point, Patrone, before I lose interest."

Victor placed a white envelope in the center of the Formica

table. "Sit down." Bosky eased back into the booth. Once he was seated, Victor continued. "I have a client in the amateur porn business. He consistently purchases a lot of product for parties, location shoots, and other venues. I've gotten to know him well."

"Isn't that special," interrupted the officer. "Scum associating with scum."

Victor ignored the comment. "John's always scouting for new talent. Believe it or not, college campuses have been his premier hunting grounds. The more prestigious the institution, the more prospects available for recruitment. Something about 'the more intellectually stimulated the mind becomes, the more liberation is expressed through the body.' *His* words, not mine. I believe your daughter is a sophomore at Vanderbilt this year, correct?"

Bosky hesitated to answer; his mind was taking a moment to connect the dots. "You bastard."

"Relax, Lieutenant. It's not as bad as it seems," Victor reassured him. "We're at ground zero here, so it's still possible to avert disaster. Apparently, Ashley met one of John's associates at a frat party. They hit it off well, and she posed for a few photos for him a couple of weeks later. Now, under normal circumstances, the way the scheme plays out is that the associate uses the photos he already has in his possession to emotionally blackmail the coed into more and more risqué behavior. Before you know it, another strung-out porn star is born."

Bosky gritted his teeth. "Those the photos?" He pointed to the envelope.

"Yes. Go ahead. Take a look."

The officer grabbed the envelope, took a deep breath, and opened it.

"I took the liberty of having strategic areas blurred out," Victor said. "I might not be a father, but I do have a sense of decency."

Bosky shook his head while flipping through several

bare-breasted photos of his daughter in provocative poses. "I can't believe this. How do I know these weren't Photoshopped?"

Victor shrugged. "You don't. But do you really want to take that kinda chance with your daughter? The question you should be asking is whether or not Ashley is susceptible to emotional blackmail."

The stunned look on Bosky's face told Victor that he was hitting close to home.

"Given your background in law enforcement," Victor continued, "I suspect there weren't a lot of Kodak moments on the home front. So I'm gonna say your answer to my offer is an emphatic yes. Here's the deal: I'll intercede on your behalf in exchange for twenty percent of all future proceeds. This guy John is in hock to me for a brick of cocaine. You pay, I lean, and Ashley continues to live a peaceful existence at Vanderbilt."

"And if I don't comply?"

Victor leaned back in the booth. "That won't happen. I'm counting on your natural instinct to protect your daughter to keep you in check."

Bosky didn't press for any further details.

"And just in case you're wondering, *Why me?*" Victor added. "Well, why not you? You've just been promoted to lieutenant, and you've got your police pension. As far as I'm concerned, everything else, which includes your service to us, is gravy. Just be thankful I'm not taking you for a helluva lot more."

Bosky stuffed the envelope inside his jacket. "Fair enough, Patrone, but just remember, the careless shepherd makes an excellent dinner for the wolf."

Victor laughed. "And who's the wolf?"

"That remains to be seen," Bosky said, standing. "Life has a funny way of working things out."

"Whatever," Victor said with a roll of his eyes. "Just make

sure the cops put pressure on the Southside Locos and my men are free and clear to do what we've got to do."

Bosky acknowledged the directive with a nod then left the diner.

Victor leaned forward to finish his iced tea. *Shepherds and wolves,* he thought. *Yet another reason to retire to a nice island in the South Pacific. Sheesh, the characters I have to put up with.*

He reached into his wallet and pulled out a hundred-dollar bill. He placed it on the table, wrote his phone number on it, then slid it underneath his plate. He eased out of the booth then headed out of the diner. *She'll call in a day or two. They always do.*

Out on the street, he pulled out his cell phone and hit speed dial. The phone rang several times before a woman answered.

"Hello," a familiar voice said.

"Hey, girl, can you meet me in my suite at the Chateau Regency later today?"

"Sure thing. What's up?"

"Not much. I'm just really wound up and need to relax."

"Oh, poor baby. I'll see what I can do," the woman said. "How's an hour sound?"

"Make it two. I got one more thing to take care of."

"Two it is.

"I look forward to seeing you," Victor said.

"I know," the woman cooed. "Keep bringin' the cash, and you'll have a generous supply of ass."

The line went dead.

CHAPTER THREE

The Compound occupied all three floors of an abandoned luxury hotel built in 1920. Formerly known as the Hanover, it had been the premier hotel in Parkbridge in its day, with numerous parties, formal balls, and other social events held there. The hotel had even been rumored to have had two former state governors sign the register as guests during its sixty years of operation.

In 1980, the Hanover was officially closed to the general public. The family of the original proprietor, Edmund Drexel, sold the hotel to Randolph & Associates and reopened it several years later. Under their management, the Hanover experienced a brief renaissance and flourished. By the mid 1990s, ownership changed hands once again. This time, however, the hotel had failed to sustain a substantial profit margin and was foreclosed on by Parkbridge National Bank & Trust Company in 1997.

With the subprime mortgage crisis in full swing, an overabundance of commercial properties had been added to the bank's real estate ledger. To alleviate this problem, PNB&T officials targeted prospects with fluid capital. The ability to close quickly and finance entire transactions independently made these clients a godsend. These dire circumstances had allowed Gemini Cordoza to purchase the former luxury hotel at well below market value.

Over the past century, the hotel had undergone numerous renovations at the expense of its various owners. At first glance, the inside looked like any other lodging facility, with a lobby, dining area, and conference suites. The current living arrangements there, however, were a different matter: junior associates and contracted help made due with conventional rooms on the ground floor, while senior associates occupied suites on the second. The third-floor penthouse was reserved for Gemini Cordoza and his guests. All the rooms came furnished with a microwave, refrigerator, and flat-screen television. In addition, Internet access was provided via a state-of-the-art wireless network.

Cordoza maintained a full-time staff of eight to oversee the Compound's day-to-day operations. They included a chauffeur, chef, housekeeper, receptionist, groundskeeper, two waiters, and a front-house manager. Any additional services that were required usually were contracted out. With most of the staff working on Nikki's "back on the block" party, today the Compound was abuzz with activity.

The dining area was plastered with welcome back, nikki signs. Balloons and ceiling danglers hung from overhead, in sharp contrast with the room's mahogany paneling and impressionistic art. Several guests had gathered over by the portable stage near the band. After four clicks from the drummer's sticks, the cover band erupted into a smooth rendition of Katrina and the Waves' "Walking on Sunshine." The song's upbeat tempo resonated throughout the hotel. Some began to dance, while other, more conservative onlookers, tapped their toes to the beat.

Nikki entered the dining area, where she exchanged hugs and kisses with the eight-member Compound staff before being ushered over to Big Al.

"Nicola," the now-slim tailor greeted her, preferring to use the formal version of her name, even though it was in fact "Nicole." "How's the dress?"

Nikki stared at Big Al's physique in surprise. "Oh, wow, is that you?"

"The one and only, darling."

"How much have you lost? You're so tiny."

"A hundred and twenty pounds," he answered proudly. "Gastric bypass."

"You look fantastic." She reached out to where Big Al's stomach used to be. He met her hand halfway then guided it toward his abdomen.

"I have a couple more surgeries left to get rid of the excess skin."

Nikki smiled. "I'm sure you'll be chiseled by next summer."

"For ten grand, I'd better be, even if they have to airbrush the muscle definition in."

The two laughed together and embraced. "Thank you for my dress, Al," Nikki whispered. "I absolutely love it."

Big Al grinned. "Anything for you."

Nikki made her way through the crowd when Spence approached her from the side, grasped her hand, and escorted her up to the stage.

"What's going on?" she protested.

The well-dressed criminal kept moving with her in tow. At the stage, Spence made eye contact with the band's lead singer and gave her a nod. "Relax, Nikki. Just go with this."

The music trailed off to a few soft chords played in the background while several white-jacketed waiters served the crowd Pinot Noir in long-stemmed wineglasses.

Spence walked onstage toward the lead singer, who handed him the microphone and stepped back. "It's a delight to host this fun-loving group surrounding me today," he announced. The crowd cheered in response. "Now for the moment we've all been waiting for. Put your hands together, and let's welcome our colleague and friend, Nikki Frank." Nikki stepped forward to the

sound of thunderous applause. The chants of her name embold-
ened her step. She waved back to the crowd. "Nikki and I met
skimming ATMs," Spence continued. "She was a skilled, street-
reputable skimmer, and I was a naïve criminal looking to expand
his trade by learning the craft. Four years ago, we were caught
tampering with a few cash machines. When the police moved in
to make the bust, we split. Nikki was arrested and sent upstate.
Today she stands before us a free woman." The audience whis-
tled and clapped. "Please join me in raising your glasses to cel-
ebrate her release." A waiter on standby presented Spence with a
glass of red wine, which he held in the air. He waited a moment
for the crowd to do the same before continuing. "No greater sacrifice does a person make than to set aside a portion of his or her
life for friends. For to sacrifice is to love. To the spirit of self-sac-
rifice! To Nikki Frank!" Spence emptied the glass of its contents
then handed it back to the waiter.

The lead guitarists played the opening chords to Diana Ross's
"I'm Coming Out." The drummer and lead singer soon joined in
on the impromptu riff. The popular song got the crowd clapping
in unison.

Spence leaned in toward Nikki. Startled, she jumped back.

"Relax," he said. "I'm not trying to make a move. I just
wanted to make sure you could hear me."

"Oh," Nikki replied, unconvinced. *I saw the way you were
leering at me in the limo, Spence.*

"Come on," he urged in a serious tone. "Cordoza is waiting
for us in the conference suite."

Nikki shrugged. *I guess that means no festivities.*

"This way," Spence directed. "Hopefully we won't run
into Lacey."

Spence and Nikki made their way past the glass-enclosed
veranda and down a corridor to the opposite side of the Compound.
When they reached the conference suite, they heard muffled

screams. Spence hesitated to knock on the door. Concerned, Nikki looked at him. His hand hovered over the oak paneling for a few seconds before he knocked three times. No answer.

"Perhaps we should come back another time, a better time," Nikki suggested.

Spence shook his head.

Another scream sounded.

He opened the door then stepped aside, motioning for Nikki to move forward. "After you."

Nikki sneered. *Wuss.*

Inside the suite stood a grand boat-shaped conference table surrounded by twenty oversize leather chairs. Up front, tied to one of them, was a partially conscious brunette with a make-shift gag hanging loose around her neck. She was dressed like a businesswoman: charcoal skirt and jacket, her hair pinned up. A bleached blonde in a curve-hugging, sapphire-blue, sleeveless dress stood in front of her, holding a cattle prod. Her chin-length bobbed hair and fake tan stood in sharp contrast with the color of her outfit.

Nikki's expression darkened. "What the...?"

"This isn't as bad as it looks," Spence said.

"Really." *It seems much worse.*

Before he could reply, the blonde jabbed the brunette again with the prod. The bound woman's body snapped back to life instantly.

"The active SWIFT Network code for the bank you work for," the blonde demanded.

The brunette moaned but didn't respond.

"Lacey," Spence called out to the blonde, interrupting her.

She froze.

"I told you this wouldn't be necessary."

Lacey lowered the cattle prod to her side and turned to face him. "True."

MATT LEATHERWOOD JR.

"Then what the hell are you doing?"

A smug expression flickered across her heart-shaped face. "There's a fine line between stagnation and progress, and it needed to be crossed."

Spence shook his head. "Torture? Have you lost your damn mind?"

"No," Lacey said, placing the wand on the conference table. "Just tired of waiting for one of your harebrained schemes to pan out."

"Does the boss know about this?"

Lacey snickered. "Not everything I do requires his stamp of approval."

Spence rolled his eyes. "Where is he? He wanted to meet with me pronto."

The former stripper delayed answering and approached the criminal pair with keen interest in Nikki. "Business call. Shouldn't be more than ten minutes."

"A bank executive..." Spence said, pausing to take in the full explosion of Lacey's cleavage bursting out from underneath the deep V neck of her dress. "I...umm..."

Nikki elbowed Spence in the ribs. Hard.

"Spit it out," Lacey said.

Spence paused, taking note of the discontent in her frigid blue eyes. "I can't believe this. We need to get this mess you've created cleaned up before somebody realizes this lady is missing and pieces together what we're trying to do."

"Handle it then," Lacey snapped, pointing to the door. "We girls"—she gestured to Nikki—"need some private time to get to know each other."

With a nod, Nikki indicated that it was okay for Spence to leave. "I got this."

Spence looked skeptical. "You sure?"

"Yeah." *I can handle McTitties here*, Nikki thought.

24

Spence opened the door. "Okay. I'll be nearby if you need me."

Nikki moved toward the conference table to put distance between her and Lacey.

She noticed that the bank executive had slipped into unconsciousness. The door closed behind Spence, and the two women stared at each other. "So you're the infamous Nikki Frank?" Lacey said, breaking the silence.

"That's right."

"Five years upstate? Not a word to the cops? And the sole reason for making all this possible? Or so the legend goes."

"Three years, six months, and nine days," Nikki corrected. "Yes, and perhaps."

Lacey drew her shoulders back and tilted her chin up in a regal pose. "Oh, because to hear the guys around here tell it, you're some sort of saint or something. I just had to hear it for myself, because I'm not buying it."

Nikki considered her words carefully before speaking. "Look, I'm grateful the crew holds me in high regard, but I can't control their opinions or perceptions."

"You know, a lot's changed here at the Compound since you've been gone."

Nikki raised an eyebrow. "Like what?"

"Like me," Lacey replied. "I'm queen bee around here."

Nikki smirked at the arrogant revelation.

"That's the way it's been, and that's the way it's gonna be. Understand?" She stared at Nikki for several moments, scanning for any tangible sign of compliance.

"Well, Your Majesty, we have a slight problem," Nikki bluffed. "I'm back."

Lacey turned around and marched back toward the captive brunette. "You might be back, honey, but you're certainly not welcome."

Nikki chuckled, the impromptu challenge of Lacey's dominance having the desired effect. It had been a lesson well learned on cellblock eight at Shaw: always present a strong front, regardless of the situation or your true intentions.

Even so, like a swimmer caught in a rip current, Nikki found herself being sucked into something from which there was quite possibly no escape.

Cordoza entered the room. His cell phone still pressed to his ear, he strode toward Lacey while continuing his conversation. "Yes, we're interested in vying for a money-brokering contract out of New York," he reassured the voice on the other end. "I don't care what you have to do. Get me in on that reverse auction pronto, all right?"

The crew leader terminated the phone call then embraced Lacey. Cordoza's hands continued to explore the curves of her body before coming to an abrupt stop on her backside. "Oh, you drive me so crazy when you dress like this," he confessed. "What am I'm I gonna do with you? I can't keep my hands off you."

Lacey smiled halfheartedly. "We have company."

Cordoza glanced around the room, noticed Nikki, then composed himself. "My apologies...I thought we were alone."

Nikki remained silent, unsure what to say. It was the first time she had seen him since she'd been locked up. He'd lost some weight and added muscle to his upper body. In his early fifties, Cordoza had a full head of neatly combed salt-and-pepper hair. Clean-shaven and wearing khakis and a traditional navy blazer minus the tie, he could have easily passed for a run-of-the-mill business executive. Images of the past flashed through Nikki's head: working closely with Cordoza, forging letters from charitable organizations and setting up bogus PO boxes to receive donations; cloning stolen cell phones from mall patrons for future usage; and their almost kissing after a successful run of the jury-duty credit-card scam—good times. There was always a charge of energy in the air when they dealt with each other, an attraction, something they both knew and suppressed in favor of an optimal working relationship.

Cordoza stepped away from Lacey. "Nikki, it's so good to see you. Please sit down."

Nikki moved to the front of the room, where Cordoza greeted her with a hug. "I sincerely apologize for not visiting you while you were away," he said, "but my main priority, first and foremost, has always been the security of this team."

She thought about it for a second. Cordoza was right. As he was the group's leader, his loyalty had to be with the crew as a whole. No exceptions. Spence, on the other hand, was without excuse. He was her colleague and friend, and that's what hurt the most. Nikki shook her head in response to Cordoza's apology. "I appreciate your candor, Gem. Thank you."

Cordoza pulled out a chair and took a seat. The ladies followed suit: Lacey sitting to his left and Nikki to his right. "Where's Spence?" he asked. It was unclear from his tone whether or not he was being sarcastic. Lacey leaned over and whispered into his ear that Spence had stepped out for a moment to give the contracted help specific instructions as to how to release the bank officer without incident. Cordoza removed his cell phone from its case and hit speed dial. The phone rang several times before it was answered.

"Taylor."

"Get in here," Cordoza ordered. "Now."

A minute later, Spence walked back into the room, followed by two burly men. They grabbed the bank executive in the chair and rolled her out of the suite. Spence took a seat next to Nikki. Lacey cast a dirty look in their direction; Nikki smirked back.

"Now that we're all finally here," Cordoza began, "let's get down to business. Nikki, I assume Spence has brought you up to speed on our latest racket?"

"Yes." She hesitated, unsure how deep an answer Cordoza was looking for. "Money laundering, I believe."

"And the twist?"

"Developing some sort of computer program to exploit financial transactions processed through ACH, to get a leg up on the competition."

Cordoza leaned back in his leather chair. "Your thoughts?"

"Well—"

"Spence," he interrupted, "seems to think we can do it."

Spence nodded.

"It can be done, in theory," Nikki confirmed. "It's just a matter of degrees of difficulty and the timeframe."

"Mm-hmm." Cordoza glanced to his left, noticing Lacey was preoccupied with her wristwatch. "So I take that to mean a 'yes' as well?"

"Spence mentioned earlier that there are some problems with the source code. I assume things aren't moving along as smoothly as you'd like." *Which is why you want my help*, she thought.

"How soon can you take a look at Spence's work?" Cordoza pressed.

Nikki answered cautiously. "Look, I'm not even sure I want to get back on board. It was my understanding that this was just supposed to be a simple meet-and-greet, with me leaving shortly after."

Cordoza's brows pulled together at the center. "Leaving?"

Spence leaned toward the conference table to gain Cordoza's attention. "I promised her we'd take her to see her brother after fifteen minutes."

Lacey rolled her eyes then once again glanced at her high-end watch.

Spence turned to Lacey. "What?" he said. "You told me, 'Whatever it takes.' Well, Lacey, that's what it took, a promise to see her brother."

"How is Marston?" Cordoza cut in.

"It's Martin," Nikki corrected.

"I meant Martin."

"I don't know. That's why I need to go see him, among many other things I have to do."

"Like?"

"Like check in at the parole office, meet my parole officer, submit to a random drug test, find a place to live, seek gainful employment."

"Do we really even need her?" Lacey asked, sounding annoyed. "Obviously she has a lot of issues to deal with right now. There must be a handful of specialists we could hire who are just as good, if not better. Besides, hacking is a perishable skill set."

Cordoza took a deep breath and ran his hand through his hair. "Loyalty means a lot to me, and Nikki's proved hers. Besides, this is far too important for us to just let anybody in on it. We keep everything in house, for now. Understand?"

Lacey let out a sigh. "All right then."

Spence cracked a smile at her frustration.

"Hold on," Nikki said catching everyone off guard. "For the record, I've maintained my basic computing skills while educating myself on a wide variety of IT technologies and techniques written about in books and magazines readily available in the prison library. Spence can always bring me up to speed on the execution, but even if I were to come back—which I haven't ruled out at this point—there's the matter of these restrictions." She went on to explain the more difficult conditions of her parole, such as random visits to a court-approved residence by a parole officer and wage garnishment for supervision and restitution fees.

Lacey leaned in toward Cordoza and whispered something. Nikki watched closely while the two collaborated. Cordoza nodded several times, reached for his money clip, and handed Lacey several hundred dollars. "Excuse us," he said, standing up. "She has an appointment with her herbalist upstate, then off to her sister's." Cordoza helped Lacey out of her chair. She gave him a peck on the cheek then left the suite in a rush.

Cordoza sat back down. "Again, I apologize for the disruption."

"No problem," Spence replied. "I'm sure it's urgent."

Nikki remained silent. *Is it really?*

"Back to your restriction concerns," Cordoza began. "I can take care of your living arrangements and employment, pending court approval of course."

Nikki looked puzzled.

Cordoza read her expression. "When I purchased this hotel, I hired a crooked asset-protection attorney to create a well-structured foreign trust that registers several dummy corporations as its parent organization. The extensive paper trail he created conceals the true ownership of this property. It cost me a fortune but was well worth it. To the world—or anyone who comes looking—this place is owned by Carson Lancaster the third of the Myriad Conglomerate. The only problem is—"

"Lancaster doesn't exist," Nikki concluded. *Clever.*

"Oh, he exists, on paper. Anyone looking to prove otherwise will exhaust a considerable amount of time and resources. Therefore, the order preventing your association with known criminals would be null and void if you decided to join us once again. In addition, since you kept your mouth shut upstate, there's no formal link between us, at least not that law enforcement is aware of. So I don't see any reason why you couldn't move back into your old suite and list this place as your legal residence."

"And gainful employment?"

"Simple. I add you to the hotel staff payroll as a consultant."

"Consultant?" Nikki repeated in an agitated tone.

"Computer software consultant," he clarified. "Even though Carson Lancaster is signing the checks, it would be for a fairly modest amount so as not to arouse suspicion. Of course, the difference between your wages and what you're accustomed to making would be made up for with under-the-table compensation."

"I suppose," Spence cut in, "random drug testing and frequent check-ins with the parole officer would be left up to Nikki?"

Cordoza smiled. "Unfortunately there are limits to the extent of my influence. Some things will just have to do be done, and there's no way around it."

Nikki nodded.

"I want you back on my team," Cordoza said, staring directly at her. "I feel—"

The high-pitched ring of a cell phone cut him off. "That'd better be important, Spence," Cordoza warned. "The only phone that should be ringing in here is mine, and that's not the case, is it?"

Nodding, Spence quickly answered the call. "Boss, it's Willard."

"And?"

"He's ready to take Nikki to see her brother."

"Okay then."

Nikki stood. "Thank you for your hospitality, Gem." *Yeah, a day late and a dollar short*, she thought.

Cordoza rendered a short, tight smile. "Take some time. Go see Marston and get back with me in a day or so. Let me know what you decide."

CHAPTER FOUR

The Maristar 245 approached the dock slowly from its starboard side. Victor waited until the craft came to a complete stop before climbing in. He greeted the pilot then took a seat across from him. Victor noticed the man's chronic skin condition and how he attempted to hide his facial redness underneath an Atlanta Braves ball cap. He shook his head in amusement. *You gotta be kidding me. Report in. Now? I'm supposed to be running the streets, not cooped up on some sailboat, riding waves.* He hated going to see Quinn; it was a time-consuming event: a thirty-minute drive to the coast, a ten-minute wait for the launch, and a fifteen-minute ferry to the yacht.

He glanced around. The eighteen-seat-capacity powerboat was empty except for the pilot and himself. At this moment, he could have been enjoying the carnal pleasures provided by a well-skilled professional; instead he was on a boat headed to see the underboss. It didn't make any sense. He could have called in a payoff report from the diner an hour ago. *What's going on here?* he wondered. He unfolded the newspaper he'd brought with him and perused the headlines.

"Excuse me," interrupted the pilot. "I need you to put on a life jacket before we launch."

Victor put down the paper and opened up his Canali suit jacket to reveal the shoulder rig holding his Beretta.

"All righty then," the pilot said. "I guess that settles that."

Victor resumed reading while the powerboat eased into the deep. An advertisement for an upcoming event caught his attention: a government auction for items seized by drug task forces, police departments, and sheriff's departments within the tri-county area, next seventy-two hours only. General public welcome. Victor grinned. He loved attending government auctions. It gave him a chance to gather unofficial intelligence about his competition and speculate about the affects seizures might have on their operations. Although this information was of some use, the real gem was what these auctions revealed about local law enforcement. Once, Victor had attended an auction where he had purchased a set of used photocopiers for a mere six hundred dollars. With the help of a hacker, he'd accessed the hard drives using free forensic software readily available online. The result: more than fifty thousand documents detailing everything from grand jury witnesses to drug-raid targets set by priority.

These machines had become digital informants, packed with sensitive data that continued to pay rich dividends daily. Victor tore out the advertisement, folded it up, and placed it inside his jacket.

"Hold on," the pilot warned, pushing the throttle forward.

Victor gripped the seat's vinyl upholstery. The wind increased, shearing through his charcoal-black hair. The Maristar accelerated to thirty-one knots then leveled off. It took a moment for Victor to adjust. In the distance he saw the silhouette of the ship.

The Seclusion was a 160-foot motor yacht designed by De Voogt Naval Architects in Holland. She had a crew of eight and could comfortably accommodate up to twelve guests in six cabins. Powered by two Detroit 16V92 diesel engines, the Feadship could maintain a top speed of fourteen knots over a sustained period of time. At present, *The Seclusion* was anchored 7.5 nautical miles off the coast. The ship to shore distance always varied, in an effort to buy time in the event of a maritime raid by authorities.

The Maristar sliced through the water on approach, and the pilot eased off the throttle. Once the boat was at a crawl, he skillfully maneuvered the powerboat next to *The Seclusion*'s aft deck. The pilot then cut the engine and announced their arrival. As Victor stood, his knees wobbled for a moment from the freshly generated wake. He then regained his balance, grabbed his newspaper, and climbed aboard the yacht.

The abundant platform space was littered with oversize lounge chairs and a colorful array of umbrellas. Several bikini-clad women took advantage of the hot weather to sunbathe. Victor walked past two of them, stopping next to a redhead in cobalt blue lying on her stomach. "Now that you've gained my attention, perhaps we can spend some time together," he said, stooping. "Once Quinn is finished with you, of course."

"Whatever," she replied, not even bothering to glance over. "I don't frequent with the hired help."

Victor swatted the beauty on the rear end with his paper.

The redhead snapped her head to the side. "Jackass!"

"Feisty too. I like that…I like it a lot." Victor stood back up and headed to the staircase that led to the main deck. The impressive flight of glass steps linked all three decks of *The Seclusion* together. He raced up the flight until he reached the main saloon.

The saloon area incorporated a semicircular bar, a large three-sided sofa facing a flat-screen television, and an eight-person dining table in the distance. The interior design boasted a rich variety of leather finishes and stained oak that blended well with the Jerusalem-gold stone tiles. Forward of the saloon was Quinn's office.

Tony Chen, a tall Asian man with prominent Caucasian

features, cut Victor off as he approached. "Have a seat," he directed.

"Excuse me?"

"Sit," Tony said, "down."

Victor rolled his eyes. *What the...?*

"The boss doesn't want to be disturbed at this time. He'll notify me when he's ready for you."

Victor took a seat on the white sectional sofa. Quinn's door was shut, a rarity. That, in addition to Tony Chen's hostile reception, concerned him. "What's going on, TC?"

Quinn's personal bodyguard and confidant paused for a moment. His olive-green eyes glanced down to the right then shifted back toward Victor. "The underboss has a lot on his mind lately. Been stuck in the office all morning. Very few breaks, if any. Now here we are, midafternoon, and he hasn't made a peep."

"I see," Victor lied, trying to make sense of the situation. "Who's in there with him?"

Tony made a distorted facial expression then let out a sigh. "I don't know, some outside accountant and the accountant's assistant. Feinberg, Hofstra, and Associates, I think." He brushed a speck of lint from the sleeve of his black Mandarin jacket. "No, it's Feinberg, Hoffman, and Associates. I stand corrected."

"Feinberg, Hoffman, and Associates," Victor repeated. "Never heard of 'em."

Tony shrugged. "That makes two of us."

"Don't we usually go with Goldstein, Rosenbaum, and Wailey out of New York?"

"Yeah," Tony said, holding up a finger. "Excuse me. Need to get situation reports from the security detail."

Victor nodded. Tony grabbed his Motorola phone from his hip, activated the direct-connect feature commonly used in dispatch radio systems, and checked in with his team for an update.

"Sorry for the disruption," he told Victor, after concluding his business. "You were saying?"

Victor rolled his eyes in frustration. "If the big boss in New York has directed us to use Goldstein, Rosenbaum, and Wailey, who the hell are Feinberg, Hoffman, and Associates?"

Tony gave the cartel lieutenant a quizzical smile. "Beats me."

Quinn's office door opened. A man with a short anchor beard and an ash-blond woman emerged. Both wore silver-gray suits with matching engraved name tags. The man paused to shake hands with Quinn. His assistant, however, continued to move forward while crunching numbers on her computer tablet. Victor stood, taking notice of her. *Not bad. Could use a little more makeup, lose the updo, and ditch the glasses.* He bit his lower lip then winked in her direction, hoping for a response. Nothing.

Quinn stuck his head out of his office. "Tony," he called out. "We need to talk."

Tony walked past the accountants and into Quinn's office. The door shut immediately. Victor glanced toward the accountant and his assistant. Their inattentiveness yielded no additional clues as to what was going on. "Excuse me," he said, breaking the silence. "Have you been with us long?"

The lead CPA looked up from the tablet he was working on. "Not particularly. New account."

Victor approached the pair from across the room. "New account? I see. And what exactly is the nature of our business together, if you don't mind my asking?"

"I don't mind you asking at all. You can ask all day, every day, but I'm not at liberty to discuss the matter. That's confidential, between my firm and Mr. Quinn, who hired us."

Victor reached into his pants pocket and pulled out two legit business cards. He gave one each to the couple. "I understand this can be a very intimidating environment for some. People tend to either be carefree or extremely guarded here. So if you change your—"

"I won't."

Victor chuckled at the accountant's assertiveness. "Our contact," he said leaning in close to the female assistant, "doesn't necessarily have to be business related, you know."

The assistant forced a halfhearted smile. The senior accountant glanced at the business card and looked up. "Mr. Patrone, you're out of line."

"Perhaps, but it wouldn't be the first time." Victor laughed at his own remark.

The senior accountant touched the small of his assistant's back and guided her forward. "Come on, Priscilla. We're out of here." The two walked across the saloon toward the glass staircase then descended the steps.

"Priscilla," Victor repeated, barely suppressing a grin. *With a name like that, probably hasn't been laid in a year or two. Definitely needs some lovin' feelin'.*

The door to the office opened once again. "Patrone!" Quinn barked.

The sound of his name being called startled him. He walked toward the office and stepped inside. The off-white carpet with burgundy specks tied in nicely with the adobe-colored walls and the sunset-cherry furniture in the cabin.

Quinn sat behind a vast executive desk in a high-back leather chair large enough to accommodate his girth. He was a bald man with a slender goatee and a sterling-silver squared diamond stud protruding from his left ear. To his left sat Tony in a matching guest chair. A wispy trail of smoke spiraled up and throughout the room: incense burning from a nearby ceramic tray.

Victor stopped several paces short of Quinn's desk. "Bosky accepted the ten grand and agreed to run interference for us. We've hit the ground running on collections. I put the word out to all street-level dealers to have their dough ready for pickup within forty-eight hours—seventy-two at the max—or suffer the repercussions."

"Excellent," Quinn replied. "Have a seat."

"Thank you." Victor sat down in a chair next to the door, against the wall.

"As you know," Quinn continued, "our boss, Francisco, is expecting the business proceeds from last quarter to be laundered to him in New York on time. Nothing new—we do it four times a year. What you don't know…"

Victor leaned forward in his chair.

"…is that he also has called for an organization-wide audit. Reports from underbosses in Miami, Columbia, and Charlotte indicate that Francisco's auditors swoop in fast, are very thorough, and don't miss a thing. Manny, in Atlanta, woke up to a team of accountants at his Windsor Heights doorstep before he even had the chance to eat breakfast."

Victor took a deep breath; the sandalwood emanating from the ceramic tray was burning his nostrils. "Damn."

"Damn is right. Looks like the big boss is going up and down the eastern seaboard. We could be next for an impromptu audit."

"And Feinberg, Hoffman, and Associates?"

Quinn smiled. "My personal assurance that all my affairs are in order. I don't want any surprises, especially at the last minute."

"Why this? Why now?" Victor shifted position in his chair, waiting for a response.

"Recession, economic uncertainty…call it what you want, but everybody's feeling the pinch, from CEOs all the way down to bums on the street. Times are tough."

"No disrespect here," Tony said, cutting into the conversation, "but underbosses have it easy. All they have to worry about is the metropolitan area where they operate and the people under their charge. Francisco, on the other hand, has to account for the entire East Coast and answer to the South Americans. Big difference."

Quinn stared at Tony. His prolonged eye contact prompted the bodyguard to speak.

"Like I said, No disrespect, boss"

"None taken." The underboss leaned back in his chair and stroked the sides of his goatee. "Patrone..." Victor perked up. "...the situation with Francisco isn't why I called you in." Quinn exchanged a look of apprehension with Tony. "I need you to do me a favor."

Victor raised an eyebrow. "Favor?"

Quinn stood up, turned around, and opened a glass-paneled door to an overhead storage cabinet behind his desk. The reflective surface of the paneling displayed a distorted image of his pinstriped suit and tie. Quinn removed several books from the shelf to reveal a digital keypad. He quickly entered a five-digit code then turned the handle of the safe to the right. Once the door opened, he removed fifteen thousand dollars: 150 hundred-dollar bills banded together into three five-thousand-dollar bundles.

Quinn returned to his desk. "That's right," he replied. "A favor."

"Umm...sure," Victor said, uncertain what to think. "What is it?"

"Emma's birthday is next week. I need you to make a charitable donation in her name to..." He ruffled through the papers on his desk until he found a pink Post-it note. "...Paris Oaks Assisted Living Facility."

Victor considered his words carefully before speaking. "Do you think that's wise? I mean, with all this stuff going on?"

"I don't see why not. This is from my own personal stash. It in no way factors into anything Francisco may or may not be doing."

"Okay, so why not write a check?"

Quinn exchanged looks with Tony once again. The bodyguard sat motionless while rolling a coin across his knuckles. Quinn shifted his attention back to Victor. "Some people in this city wouldn't cash a check from me to save their lives. Emma is one such person. The minute she sees my personal information in the top left-hand corner of that slip, she'll do everything in her power to see to it that the money is returned. She wouldn't want her coworkers at Paris Oaks, or anybody for that matter, aware of our connection."

Victor nodded.

"You know she doesn't approve of the business I'm in or the lifestyle I lead."

"Yet you persist." *Fool.*

"What can I say? I love her."

Victor gestured toward the stack of money with an open hand. "Cash? Really? You can't get a money order? Put it on a prepaid Visa? Get a bank draft or something?"

Quinn sighed. "I ask you to pay off a dirty cop, and you got no problem. I ask you to make a charitable donation, now you got problems. What gives?"

"No problem," Victor said with a shrug. "Just seems out of the ordinary is all."

"Well, these are extraordinary circumstances. I'm under a lot of stress here. So please take care of this for me." Quinn grabbed the money and held it out.

Victor stood and approached the desk. "Fine." He grabbed the stacks of cash and stuffed them inside his jacket. "Anything else?" *Hope not*, he thought.

Quinn glanced at Tony. "Not at this time."

"Good," Victor said, as he headed to the door.

Tony placed his coin back in his pocket, stood, and followed him out of the office.

CHAPTER FIVE

Willard opened the passenger door from the outside. "Ms. Frank," he called out, extending his arm to assist her out of the limousine.

Nikki stepped out of the Chrysler. "Thank you."

"My pleasure. Are you sure you don't want me to stick around and wait? I'm at your disposal."

Nikki cupped her hand and tucked her auburn hair behind her ear. "Thanks, but that won't be necessary. I don't know how long I'll be or where I'm headed after this."

"Very well." Willard handed her a folded newspaper with thirty dollars on top. "The paper you requested earlier."

Nikki stared at the crisp bills. "What's this?"

"Lunch money. I heard you didn't get a chance to eat at the Compound."

"I couldn't," she replied, handing the money back. "Besides, the prison provided me with a twenty-dollar stipend."

Willard pushed her hand away. "Take it. You can't get a decent meal in this town for that."

"All right." Nikki pulled her arm back down to her side and crumpled the bills in her hand. "If you insist."

"I do." Willard walked back around the limousine to the driver's side.

"Thank you."

"You're welcome, Ms. Frank."

Nikki watched as the chauffeur got back in the limo and pulled into traffic. She stuffed the money down her bra and entered the main office of the assisted-living facility.

The empty waiting room was filled with Queen Anne–style furniture: a sofa with matching coffee table, two club chairs, and a love seat. A russet area rug covered most of the floor space; its large floral pattern coordinated surprisingly well with the oxblood-red furnishings. welcome to paris oaks in mustard-gold lettering was emblazoned on the wall directly behind the receptionist.

The young redhead was oblivious to Nikki's approach.

"Good afternoon," Nikki said.

The woman looked up from behind her computer screen. "Good afternoon. Welcome to Paris Oaks Assisted Living Facility. How can I help you?"

"I'm here to see Marty Frank."

The receptionist opened her top drawer and removed a clipboard with a form and pen attached. "Not a problem. I just need you to fill this out and bring it back up to me with your driver's license."

Nikki grabbed the clipboard and took a seat on the sofa. A few minutes later, she had completed the form and was at the front desk. "Excuse me."

"Yes," the woman replied, not bothering to look up.

"I have a slight problem."

"Yes, ma'am. What would that be?"

"I…" Nikki hesitated. "…don't exactly have a driver's license."

The receptionist stopped what she was doing and made direct eye contact with her. "Well, that *is* a problem."

Nikki handed the clipboard back. The receptionist took it then glanced over the information provided. "Ms. Frank, if you'll have a seat, I'll be more than happy to see if I can help resolve this matter for you."

Nikki forced a smile.

The woman picked up the phone and dialed a number. Moments later, an older Hispanic woman emerged from one of the back offices. Nikki recognized her: Laura Ruiz, the facility director. In her past dealings with her, the welfare of the family and her mother's illness had taken priority. This time it would be about her and what she wanted. Mrs. Ruiz hadn't changed much in five years: backcombed outgrown pixie hairstyle, sagging jowls with excessively caked-on makeup, and Corinne McCormack reading glasses suspended around her neck by an elegant cord. Nikki stood to greet her. "Mrs. Ruiz—"

"I've been expecting you," Mrs. Ruiz interrupted her. "Come with me."

The director made an abrupt turn and headed back in the opposite direction. Nikki followed. The two women entered an executive office decorated with elegant but modest furniture. Mrs. Ruiz circled around her desk and took a seat. "We need to talk," she said. "Please have a seat."

Nikki complied. "What's going on?"

"The Department of Corrections notified me of your release earlier today. We here at Paris Oaks weren't sure when you'd show up, but we knew you would."

"Well, I'm here. Now how is that a concern of the Department of Corrections?"

"It's not," Mrs. Ruiz said. "However, it is a concern of mine."

Nikki crossed her legs and waited for an explanation.

"Have you heard of the Hernandez Act or state statute 11825?"

Nikki shook her head, unsure where this was going.

Mrs. Ruiz donned her reading glasses and began typing on her keyboard. A couple of minutes later, she stopped, adjusted her screen, and silently read over its contents. "About a year and a half into your sentence," she began, "a man named Alberto Hernandez went to visit his mother in an Atlanta area nursing home. While there, he tried to settle a long-time dispute between his mother and two other residents over a hairbrush. The situation escalated, and he stepped outside, removed a two-foot stake from the ground, and severely beat the other two women with it. They were eighty-one and sixty-four years old."

Nikki's jaw dropped. "You've gotta be kidding me."

"Both women suffered severe trauma and broken bones. The investigation later revealed that Hernandez was a career criminal with a violent past. As a result, the state legislature enacted statute 11825, which requires all visitors at special care facilities to—"

"To provide some sort of identification, such as a driver's license," Nikki finished for her.

"Correct." Mrs. Ruiz looked up from her computer. "We then take the ID, log in to the state's database, and check for a criminal background. The Department of Corrections is obligated to notify all facilities statewide of current and pending offender releases, so we're already aware of your criminal background. This brings us to an impasse."

Nikki raised an eyebrow. "An impasse?"

"Yes. You want to see Marty, and I'm legally bound, as director of this facility, to protect him along with all the other residents here. An impasse. Anyone with a criminal background needs to be properly vetted by the state before visiting with any of the residents here at Paris Oaks."

"So you're telling me I can't see my own brother because some whack job took out two elderly women?"

Mrs. Ruiz clasped her hands. "One of those elderly women happens to be the mother of the current lieutenant governor."

Nikki was annoyed. "I can't believe this."

"You can see your brother at any time," Mrs. Ruiz reassured her. "Once you've been vetted."

"Vetted?"

"By the state's violent-offender assessment committee. It's a six-member panel, consisting of a judge and five other political appointees. You submit a packet for review, and then they look it over and take into account your criminal record, your conduct while incarcerated, and any other information provided by persons on your behalf. Then they make a decision. If it's favorable, you're clear for six months before having to repeat the process."

"How long does this usually take?" Nikki asked.

"Sixty to ninety days, depending on the workload."

Nikki looked up at the ceiling and blinked several times. "Unbelievable," she muttered, shaking her head. *And you won't cut me any slack because you're a by-the-book bitch.*

"You're welcome to retain legal counsel," Mrs. Ruiz suggested. "I hear it expedites the process."

"That's not an option for me at the moment."

Mrs. Ruiz frowned.

"So how do I get started?" Nikki asked.

"Meet with your parole officer and mention that you'd like to submit an offender-assessment packet to the state board."

Nikki uncrossed her legs and stood. "Bureaucracy," she huffed.

Mrs. Ruiz paused. "Excuse me, miss, but we're not finished yet."

"Oh." Nikki sat back down.

Mrs. Ruiz rifled through her top desk drawer and removed a manila folder. "There's the matter of finances to discuss." She opened up the file and removed a spreadsheet. After glancing over the numbers for a moment, she handed the document to Nikki. "As you can see, your mother's trust fund is projected to be depleted within the next thirty to ninety days."

Nikki gaped at the estimated projections. *This can't be right.*

A grim look swept across Mrs. Ruiz's face. "With that said," she began, her voice cold and distant, "we'll need an additional source of funding if Marty is to remain a resident of this facility."

"Wait a minute," Nikki protested. "I thought there was at least ten years' worth of funds set aside for him?"

"In the beginning, there was." Mrs. Ruiz leaned back in her chair to stretch. "However, your late mother initially enrolled your brother in our facility under the government health-care subsidy option."

Nikki stared at Mrs. Ruiz for a moment then scrunched her forehead up in confusion. "English, please."

"The health-care subsidy option provides a guaranteed set amount of money, based on current interest rates, to help provide for Marty's care. However, since this is a private facility, the government mandates that individual funds must be utilized first before receiving the subsidy. With recent economic developments, fluctuating interest rates, and several facility fee hikes over the years, monthly deductions from the trust continually adjusted as well. Some months it was higher; some months it was lower, but the government contribution remained steady. This created a situation that accelerated the depletion of funds."

A worried look poured over Nikki's face. "How much are we talking here?"

"Roughly, about six thousand a month for room and board," Mrs. Ruiz said.

"Six thousand a month!" Nikki dug her fingers into the newspaper Willard had given her.

The sound of the crumpling paper garnered the director's attention. "I know it's a lot. Your mother would have been better off not selecting the health-care subsidy option. The money would've lasted longer." Mrs. Ruiz broke eye contact with Nikki and glanced down at her desk. "Nothing personal. Merely stating facts here."

"What was she thinking?"

The director looked back up, surprised. "Your mother had a lot on her mind—that's what she was thinking: the terminal cancer diagnosis, preparing her estate, Marty, you. She did the best she could with the time she had left."

"Yeah, but it's still a mess I'll have to clean up."

"As I recall, you weren't exactly rushing over to attend the client-family support meetings with the case officer," she reminded her. "Your input could've been provided then, during the methods and sources of financing session."

An uncomfortable feeling lodged itself in the pit of Nikki's stomach. "Business," she admitted, forcing herself to look around instead of at Mrs. Ruiz. *You wouldn't understand*, she thought.

"Ah, yes, business," Mrs. Ruiz continued in a mildly condescending tone. "When we first met several years ago, I recall you had a nice, cushy job with the government in DC. You returned to Parkbridge, started associating with unsavory characters and running the streets at all hours of the night, and now you sit before me a convicted felon. What happened?"

Nikki rolled her eyes. "It's complicated."

"It usually is." Mrs. Ruiz tugged on her Chanel jacket then looked back up. The emotionless shield drained from her face. "Honey, does it involve a man?"

"I'd rather not talk about it," Nikki insisted.

"Relationships are messy," Mrs. Ruiz stated in a self-critical tone. "That's their nature. They start messy, and they end messy. Women just happen to be along for the ride. So if it's a man— and I suspect it is—now's the time to leap from that speeding train before it reaches its final destination."

Nikki laughed. "No, it's not a man. Believe me."

Mrs. Ruiz leaned back in her chair. "If you say so, darling, but in my experience, only a man can take you further than you want to go and keep you longer than you want to stay. Besides,

MATT LEATHERWOOD JR.

the changes you've undergone over the last four to five years since we last met have 'man' written all over them."

For a moment the two sat still, staring at each other. Finally, Mrs. Ruiz broke her gaze and picked up the phone. She pressed the intercom button then dialed extension 242. "Bethany, send in Ms. Daniel."

The door to the office opened. A petite baby-faced brunette, clutching a handheld radio, entered the room.

"Nikki, this is Ms. Daniel," Mrs. Ruiz said. "She's Marty's mental health worker."

The two women smiled at each other then shook hands.

Mrs. Ruiz glanced at her wristwatch. "It's midafternoon. The residents of C dorm are out right now."

"That's correct, ma'am," Ms. Daniel confirmed. "The bus departed an hour ago. Everyone was present and accounted for."

"Wonderful." Mrs. Ruiz removed her reading glasses and massaged her temples. "I don't know why I'm even considering this, but everyone deserves a little mercy extended to them from time to time."

Nikki perched on the edge of her seat.

Mrs. Ruiz let out a sigh. "Ms. Daniel, please give Ms. Frank here a quick tour of C dorm as well as Marty's room."

"Yes, ma'am."

"Keep it brief and the conversation focused on generalities. You are not to discuss medical ailments, medications being administered, behavioral issues, or treatment plans. As far as health information privacy is concerned, we're walking a fine line here. Until Ms. Frank is properly vetted, you'll treat her like a stranger without a need to know."

Ms. Daniel nodded. "Understood."

Nikki stood and followed the young woman to the door. "Thank you, Mrs. Ruiz."

"You're welcome," she said, "but I didn't do it for you. I'm

48

doing it out of respect for your late mother. It's the only reason I even entertained this idea."

Nikki forced a smile.

"You ready?" Ms. Daniel asked.

"I am."

The two women left the office together, walked back toward the waiting room, then headed across the facility grounds toward the dormitories.

"How's Marty doing?" Nikki asked.

"Good, real good," Ms. Daniel answered. "He's very popular here with the staff."

The facility worker picked up her pace; Nikki adjusted to gain ground. "Any friends?"

"Chip and Wally. The three are virtually inseparable."

They walked past a pay phone near the main parking lot then continued for about a hundred yards before coming to a stop at a large ranch-style building. Ms. Daniel unlocked the main door. "Here we are."

"Is this place new?" Nikki gazed at the sizable structure for a moment. "I don't remember it from any of my previous visits."

"It's somewhat new, about three years old now."

Ms. Daniel cut on the lights and motioned for Nikki to enter the building. "This is the main lounge and game room area."

Nikki looked around. There was an air hockey table, several sofas and lounge chairs, an electronic shooting basketball game, and two billiards tables.

"And school? What about school?" Nikki inquired. She was aware that her brother's special education program had ended when he turned twenty-four, a decade ago. Marty now required continuous living-skills instruction.

"He enjoys the independent living skills curriculum taught here. Loves to mop floors, despises doing laundry, and is still a bit confused about the iron and how it works."

Nikki chuckled. She recalled the number of shirts Marty had destroyed over the years while holding the appliance too long against the fabric. Even when he was supervised, his inability to correctly judge time had disastrous consequences.

The pediatric behavioral health specialist, assigned to the family early on, had explained that Marty suffered from Down syndrome. With an intellectual disability that was in the mild to moderate range, he wasn't expected to progress at the same rate as Nikki. Over time, the intellectual and emotional gap between the two siblings widened, creating a situation in which the younger child, Nikki, eventually became her brother's caregiver. She resented this prognosis from the beginning—always having to explain to others his genetic disorder, working extra hard so as not to appear to be taking her own abilities for granted, and never having enough time to engage her own personal pursuits and hobbies. Down syndrome had become a centerpiece in her family. It wasn't until Nikki was an adult that she realized Marty had added a special dimension to her life. It was the realization that you accommodate other people not by going out your way but by realizing "the norm" is a midpoint, not a requirement.

The women moved on, walking through the lounge, past the dining area, and toward the laundry room. Next to the wash area were the communal restroom and showers. Ms. Daniel made a left there and continued down the residential wing until she reached Marty's room.

Stepping inside, she flipped on the light switch. Nikki gasped in amazement. A giant wallpaper mural poster of Cam Newton above the bed came to life. The Carolina Panther quarterback appeared to be leaping over one of his own lineman while dodging two Arizona Cardinal defensive backs. The walls were painted a cross between gray and beige, and a Panther team rug extended from beneath the bed toward the door. The room had a cozy, welcoming feel and was far from drab. *This is so Marty*, Nikki thought. "I love what you've done with the place," she commented.

Ms. Daniel beamed with pride. "Thank you, we try to personalize each residents room according to their preferences."

A strong aroma evoked a sense of familiarity. Nikki inhaled to try to determine the scent. "Is that—"

"Bubble gum?" Ms. Daniel answered, anticipating the question. "Yes, it is. Actually, it's bubble-gum fragrance oil. Keeps the room smelling fresh and the residents calm. We have several versions, from apple pie to vanilla wafer. Different residents prefer different scents. Believe it or not, it actually helps suppress appetite too, much to the approval of our staff dietician."

Ms. Daniel moved toward the bed; Nikki followed. The mental health worker pointed out the blue-and-black Carolina Panthers team comforter with matching sheets and pillow: a Christmas gift to Marty from the facility staff, she explained.

Nikki lowered her head. "I...umm..." she stuttered. "I sent letters. Did..."

Ms. Daniel leaned over, set her radio on the nightstand, and opened the top drawer. She removed two bundled stacks of letters. "Whenever I worked the night shift, I read one of your letters to Marty before he turned in for the night."

She handed Nikki one of the stacks of correspondence.

Nikki let out a sigh of relief. "Thank you," she said. She thumbed through the letters quickly. On all the envelopes, the prison's return address had been blotted out with black ink. She showed a few of the envelopes to Ms. Daniel.

"Per Mrs. Ruiz's instruction," Ms. Daniel explained. "The staff here has always maintained that you've been away on business. To acknowledge otherwise would create an unnecessary stressor in Marty's life. As you probably know, stressors have the potential to trigger challenging behavior in persons with Down syndrome."

Nikki completely understood the reasoning and didn't press the issue any further. She wandered over to the dresser. Numerous photos lined the inside perimeter of the mirror.

"Pictures from various outings," Ms. Daniel commented.

Nikki took a closer look. There was a snapshot of Marty at Bank of America Stadium with a smiling Cam Newton, another of him with several professional cheerleaders, and one with him and two men she presumed were Chip and Wally. She skipped over more pictures to the opposite side of the mirror: Marty eating pizza with Ms. Daniel, Marty opening Christmas gifts, and Marty with their late mother, Nancy, at the hospital several months before her death six years ago.

Another photo grabbed Nikki's attention. She reached up and removed it. *Where have all the years gone?* she wondered. *One minute you're a happy young adult in a nuclear family, and the next, you're a convicted felon, estranged from your family and friends.*

"What is it?" Ms. Daniel asked.

Nikki ignored the question, drawing the photo closer to herself. "It's one of the last times my family was all together, fall of 2000."

Ms. Daniel moved alongside Nikki to get a better look at the image: the entire Frank family was standing on the porch of their Southern-style two-story home.

"There's Dad in his dress blues," Nikki pointed out. "Mom, healthy and happy. I love that conservative evening gown she wore to the marine corps ball that year. She looks so elegant. Marty, of course, is holding the pumpkin, and there's me, standing next to him."

Ms. Daniel smiled.

Nikki looked over at her. "Good times, before it all fell apart. A year later, Dad was killed in Afghanistan. Eight months after that, my mother's cancer was diagnosed. When her health insurance coverage ran out, she was forced to sell her home to pay for more aggressive forms of treatment. It was hell."

The corners of Ms. Daniel's lips turned downward. "I'm sorry to hear that," she said, lowering her eyes.

Nikki placed the picture back in the crevice of the mirror. "I can't believe he still has this."

"Why do you say that?"

She smiled. "Seems kinda of silly now, but I wanted to take this photo to show my sorority sisters the type of gown I had in mind for our annual ball. Marty wouldn't part with it, though—his OCD was in full effect, even after I assured him that I'd bring it right back. He wouldn't budge. We fought for two days, and during each encounter, he threw a massive tantrum. Finally, I just had another print made."

Ms. Daniel nodded. "Not to get into specifics, but I know what you mean. I've experienced that behavior with him on many occasions: consistent obsessive-compulsive disorder. It's a comorbidity to his Down syndrome. When Marty fixates on something, especially something given directly to him, there's no such thing as a return, regardless of the situation. In his mind, it's his, plain and simple."

Nikki smiled slightly. "Isn't that the truth?"

The handheld radio on the nightstand crackled; Nikki recognized Mrs. Ruiz's voice. "Ms. Daniel, come in. Over."

She grabbed the radio and pushed the "transmit" button. "Ms. Daniel here. Go ahead."

"Dispatch just called. The residents of C dorm are on their way back from training. Please escort Ms. Frank back to the main office."

"Understood. Out."

"Training?" Nikki said. "What kind of training?"

"Special Olympics," Ms. Daniel replied. "Twice a year, summer and winter games."

"What does Marty do?"

Ms. Daniel moved back toward the bedroom door. "Soccer during the summer games and floorball in the winter."

A look of confusion draped across Nikki's face, making her eyebrows dip toward each other. "Floorball?"

"Think indoor hockey for five, plus a goalie."

"And his positions?" Nikki asked.

"Center in floorball," Ms. Daniel said, cutting off the lights. "And designated team shooter in soccer."

Nikki smiled. "That's so great."

Ms. Daniel motioned that she was ready to leave.

"Oh," Nikki said, removing the business section from her newspaper. "Do you have a pen I can borrow?"

"We really should be leaving now," Ms. Daniel said.

"This'll only take a second."

Ms. Daniel handed her a pen from a pocket in her blouse.

"Thank you." Nikki glanced over the main article of the business section and circled the third word in each of the first three paragraphs of the story. When she finished, she handed the pen back to Ms. Daniel, tucked the business section under her arm, and disposed of rest of the newspaper in a nearby trash can. "Ready," she announced.

"Follow me then."

The two women left the room and made their way back up to the lounge, where they exited the dorm. They continued across the facility grounds until they reached the main parking lot.

Two yellow buses pulled onto the campus and drove by. Some of the residents waved in passing. Ms. Daniel waved back.

Nikki pointed to the nearby pay phone. "I didn't make arrangements to be picked up. I'll need to make a phone call."

"Sure, not a problem. I've got to get back to work anyway. Duty calls." Ms. Daniel extended her hand. "Nice meeting you."

Nikki shook it. "Thanks so much for the tour."

"You're welcome. I look forward to working with you in the future."

"Likewise."

The two parted ways, and Nikki made her way over to the pay phone. She picked up the handset and placed a collect call.

"Abbott Software and Technologies," a female voice announced after several rings.

Nikki pulled the business section of the paper out from underneath her arm and held it up.

"Agent 2294, day code, business section, August twenty-sixth, identification procedure."

"Proceed," the operator directed.

Nikki brought the paper into closer view to read the words circled earlier. "Starbucks, employment, private sector."

"Confirmed. How may I assist you, Special Agent?"

"Set up a meet with Harlan Fisk as soon as possible, near the place where we must all say our final good-byes. There's an abandoned warehouse half a mile from there. He'll know exactly what I'm talking about."

"Anything else?"

"Not at this time," Nikki said, then hung up.

CHAPTER SIX

Victor swiped his key card through the reader then entered his suite at the Chateau Regency. A blonde, wearing a sleeveless blue dress with a deep V neck, sat waiting for him on the sofa.

"You're late."

"Tied up," Victor replied. "Had to meet with my boss."

"That's gonna cost extra."

"Which part, being late or tied up?"

"Both."

Victor gave her a disgruntled look. *Figures.*

"If you want to play," Lacey reminded him, "you've got to pay—simple as that."

Victor moved toward the sofa. "Bondage, as much as it intrigues me, isn't my thing."

"Fair enough," Lacey said, glancing at her watch. "You have forty-five minutes left. Do you wish to continue to discuss my fees or get down to business?"

Victor smiled. "Business, of course."

Lacey stood. "All right then. I was hoping you'd say that."

Victor bit his lower lip. *Mmm, mmm, mmm.* The sight of her figure-hugging dress made it obvious that she exercised and dieted on a consistent basis.

Lacey circled around the cartel lieutenant and approached him from behind. She pressed her body up against his. The exquisite softness of her breasts made Victor groan.

"That'll be fifteen hundred dollars," she whispered into his ear.

Victor glanced over his shoulder for an explanation.

"I work on a strictly outcall basis; you should know that by now. It's your responsibility to provide the place. So that's and additional four hundred fifty dollars for the room, which my man provided unknowingly, plus an additional fifty for being late. My time is valuable."

Victor removed one of the five-thousand-dollar stacks of cash from inside his jacket and counted off the correct number of bills.

Lacey was transfixed. "Damn."

"Here," Victor said, passing the cash to her. "Now, have all debts been settled?"

Lacey took the money and recounted it. "For now."

"Good." Victor watched as she placed the notes inside a wristlet on the coffee table.

When she finished, she undressed. Victor's eyes widened at the shape and fullness of her breasts. Lacey's midriff was ripped, accentuated by the presence of a shamrock navel ring. She grabbed Victor's hand and led him to the back. He smiled, concentrating on the shifting of her delicious rear end as she walked.

"Now why don't you make yourself a little more comfortable?" she said.

Victor removed his jacket, revealing the Galco shoulder holster beneath.

Lacey grabbed the designer coat and placed it across a chair. "Third time this month. You know how to keep a gal busy."

A devilish grin lit up Victor's face. "When I find a good thing, I like to stick it."

Lacey smiled. "Well, I thank you, but more important, my bank account thanks you."

"You're well worth it. Not like the others."

"I know," Lacey said.

She caressed Victor's shoulders and neck then ran her hands down his chest next to the holster on his left side.

Victor savored the scent of her sweet perfume. "Mmm, you smell so good."

"Vanille Aoud."

"Mm-hmm."

Lacey reached out and grabbed his Beretta. Victor jerked, seizing her hand. "What do you think you're doing?"

"Do you plan on doing me again while wearing this contraption?"

Victor shook his head.

"Okay, then relax."

Victor released his grip. No one had ever touched his piece before. It was a personal rule, one he'd never violated, until now.

"Careful, I keep a round in the chamber," he warned.

Lacey disengaged the holster's retention strap and pulled the Beretta out.

"You sure you know how to handle that, cupcake?"

Lacey huffed in annoyance as she pointed the weapon to the side. "Safety off," she announced, sweeping the lever up with her thumb. Seconds later, she reversed her action. "Safety on."

"Impressive," Victor commented. "Now put that thing away before somebody gets hurt."

"Soldiers, cops, gun enthusiasts—they're all the same. The only thing they love more than me is their guns. You could say I've picked up a thing or two."

Victor cocked an eyebrow. "Like what?"

Lacey pointed the weapon back in his direction. "Does this make you nervous?"

"No," he lied. The last person to point a loaded gun at him had forfeited not only his life but also the lives of his family.

"Good." Lacey closed the distance between them, raised the Beretta to Victor's head, and traced the barrel down his cheek and along his neck.

Victor closed his eyes and focused on the strange yet exhilarating sensations flowing through his body. *Keep on moving*, he thought. *Don't stop.*

Lacey continued to trace a path across his shoulder to the center of his chest. "Tell me a secret."

"I…" He hesitated. "I wear silk underwear."

Lacey laughed. "Darling, I already know that."

Victor remained silent, unsure what to say next.

"Something else," she prompted.

"I'm in the drug trade."

She moved the Beretta in small circles against Victor's chest. "That's a start. Go on."

"I'm thinking of leaving the business," he admitted.

She gave him a puzzled look. "Why?"

"I've grown tired."

"Honey, we're all tired. No pass on that one. Try again."

"The competitive nature of the business," Victor replied. "It's getting to me. Either you move up or get tossed aside like yesterday's garbage. No middle ground. Somebody out there is always smarter, more violent, or better equipped than you. Seems like becoming a lieutenant is a lot easier than remaining one. There's an endless supply of punks out there always looking to do you in. I'm on edge twenty-four seven."

Lacey deliberately drew the weapon farther down, along Victor's abs. "Good, but you can do better."

Beads of sweat formed on his brow while he searched for something more to say.

Lacey pushed the safety into the "off" position. The audible click gained Victor's attention. "Perhaps you need some incentive," she said, stopping near his pelvis. "Now tell me a real secret."

Victor took a deep breath. "I've been stealing money from my boss," he divulged. "And I think he's on to me."

This was the first time Victor had said the words out loud. Confession never had felt so good. It was both raw and liberating. He was fully aroused now.

"Now we're getting somewhere," Lacey praised him, taking notice of his erection.

The buxom blonde put the Beretta back on "safe" and set it on top of the nightstand. "Okay, I think you're ready."

"More than you know," Victor said. He quickly got undressed and followed Lacey to the bed.

She took a seat near the edge of the mattress, set the alarm clock radio for the remaining time left, and leaned back. "Just so you know, time's up when the alarm sounds."

Victor shrugged. "Got it."

"Good," Lacey said, flinging her legs apart.

Victor grabbed her by the hips and pulled her closer to him. "You're expensive yet effective."

"Have to be," she said matter-of-factly. "Repeat business is crucial."

CHAPTER SEVEN

Nikki watched the taxi disappear down the winding road into the night. She continued up the ramp of the warehouse toward the cargo door, ducked under the partially raised gate, and entered the building. Inside, it was cold and dark. The energy-efficient lighting cast a faint glow by which to navigate. Rows of empty freight racks extended as far as Nikki could see. An open space in the distance revealed a midsize modular office constructed out of a shipping container.

Cautiously she approached it and positioned herself to the side of the door. Nikki took a deep breath then checked the handle to see if it was locked. It wasn't. She opened the door and immediately jumped.

A short, stocky man with round wire-rimmed glasses loomed in the doorway. He wore a traditional navy-blue suit, a white shirt, and a red-and-gray square-patterned tie. Gone were the off-the rack short-sleeve oxfords and tan slacks from the past, along with the wedding ring. The only thing familiar to Nikki was the man's government-regulated hairstyle. "It's about time," he said, recognizing her.

Nikki slapped him across the face. "Nice to see you too, Harlan. You should visit more often, you know."

Harlan's round face creased in pain. "Fair enough…I deserve that," he said, rubbing his cheek. "What's it been? Four years?"

"Something like that and not a single visit from you or anybody else on this task force."

Harlan removed his glasses, took out a handkerchief, and wiped them clean. "Operational security."

Nikki noticed that his former generic frames had been replaced by an expensive Matsuda version. "Operational security? Is that what you're going with?"

"Precisely. Prisons are cesspools of corruption, inhabited by snitches, opportunists, and guards on the take. The last thing I wanted to do was risk your life over a meet, just to boost your lack of self-esteem over parental abandonment issues." Harlan put his glasses back on. "Even if we used the best ruse to follow up with you, there was no guarantee you wouldn't have been made. One dead federal agent is too high a price for the Crime Enforcement Task Force to pay. We're just a provisional team sanctioned by the Justice Department and tolerated by the FBI. Don't think there aren't law enforcement bureaucrats out there who wouldn't hesitate to try to shut us down over such a tragedy."

Nikki clenched her jaw and took in a deep breath. Harlan was right. If Warden Penton could get away with viewing inmates in the nude at Shaw, anything was possible. "Why'd I have to do the extended time?" she asked. "'Eighteen months tops—that's what you said."

"You knew the risks when you were selected for the task force," Harlan reminded her. "Just be thankful you didn't have to do the whole five years."

Nikki narrowed her eyes. "Don't patronize me." *I could've handled it*, she thought.

"Fine. Have it your way." Harlan stepped aside and motioned for her to enter the office.

"Nice suit," she remarked, commenting on his new look.

Inside, another government official sat waiting at a table. Nikki stared in his direction. *Who the hell is that?* she wondered.

The bureaucrat wore the same standard suit as Harlan, however his was gray and accentuated with a blue striped tie. His shiny pate reflected a shimmer of office light.

"You wanna know why you had to do the extended time?" Harlan asked. "Meet Warren Kepler, our new regional director."

Director Kepler stood. He was a towering six foot three, a stark contrast to Harlan. In his left hand, he clutched a yellow folder labeled, "Confidential."

Nikki extended her hand in a friendly gesture.

"Sir, Special Agent Nicole Frank," Harlan said.

The two shook hands.

"Pleased to meet you, Agent Frank."

"Thank you, sir, but what happened to Director Garrett?"

"RD Garrett was promoted to Deputy Director of Undercover and Sensitive Operations, East Coast."

"Oh," Nikki said, surprised. "Well, good for him."

Harlan turned toward her. "That happened about midway through your sentence."

"Speaking of my sentence, sir, my field supervisor here tells me you'll be able to shed some light on why I had to do the extended time."

Director Kepler fidgeted with the folder in his hand. "Eighteen months seemed a little fishy...too short. Harlan and I discussed the matter when I first came on board. I felt in order for the task force to get the most mileage out of this program, you simply had to do more time."

Nikki cut a cursory glance in Harlan's direction. *Really?* she thought. *I thought you were supposed to be my advocate. You've always gone to bat for personnel in the past. What's changed?*

"Besides," the director continued, arching his eyebrows.

"With overcrowding and good behavior, you still came out earlier than expected."

Nikki let out an unintentional sigh. "That's not the point, sir."

"You're right. Backstopping your cover and making sure it was airtight was. The days of assumed identities and aliases are over. They require heavy logistical support, put agents under an enormous amount of stress, and most important, they simply don't hold up under intense scrutiny. *You* are your cover. So everything about Nicole Frank needs to scream criminal, ex-con, shady individual." Director Kepler opened the folder and glanced over the documents inside. "Now, are you ready to take on another assignment?"

Nikki balked at even responding to the question.

"Zayda Voshkie," Harlan read off a brief sheet on the table. "Forty-five, female, Armenian descent. Heavy dealings in securities fraud, money laundering, embezzlement, and wire fraud. Close ties to Russian arms dealer Yuri Abelev."

Nikki moved around the table in between the two men. "Whoa, hold on a minute. Before we get wrapped up in Zayda Ushki—"

"That's Voshkie," Harlan corrected.

Nikki tilted her head toward her field supervisor. "Voshkie, thank you."

Harlan grinned.

"We," she continued, "need to reassess and reevaluate the Cordoza crew."

Director Kepler made a disgruntled face. "The Cordoza crew? What do we want with those yahoos?"

"Besides," Harlan added, "your cover is already set. They were a means to an end: help establish your backstory. Strictly small potatoes."

Nikki shook her head. "I'm not so sure about that."

"Look, I know what this is," Director Kepler said, cutting in.

"Crossed-lives syndrome. You've been under so long that you've established formidable bonds with these people. You want to spend more time with them, live in this fictional world you've created, and dispense with your true identity."

Harlan looked Nikki over. The maize-colored cocktail dress she had on clearly caught his attention. "Perhaps that explains this prom-dress thing she's wearing, sir. Last time I checked, newly released inmates wore something a bit more plain."

"Gentlemen, I don't have crossed-lives syndrome," Nikki snapped. "What I do have is an organization that's expanded its criminal repertoire over the last four years to include sophisticated white-collar crime."

Director Kepler took a seat. "Go on."

"I was approached earlier today by Spence Taylor—"

"That's one of the lead foot soldiers for the crew, sir."

"Thank you, Harlan. Please continue, Agent Frank."

Nikki sat down. "Spence picked me up from the prison in a limo, showered me with gifts, and ushered me to a party under the guise of welcoming me back into society. This party, however, was short-lived, and I found myself witnessing the torture of a bank executive for an active SWIFT Network code. An instant later, I was in a meeting with Gemini Cordoza."

"What did they want?" Harlan asked.

"My help in the development of software that could potentially exploit the nation's Automated Clearing House payment system."

Harlan and Director Kepler stared at each other. Finally, Director Kepler spoke up. "Sounds like a job for Homeland Security, Cybersecurity Division."

"Or Secret Service," Harlan said, easing into a chair. "It's one of those jurisdictional gray areas. You've got the nation's entire cyber network and infrastructure under Homeland Security and the payment and financial systems under Secret Service."

Director Kepler nodded. "Either way it's a cluster fuck. Besides, we don't even know if the threat is credible. We're sticking with the Voshkie case."

Nikki felt Kepler was quick to dictate to subordinates but slow to question and engage senior leadership. He appeared to be super busy, very serious, and somewhat aloof. Nikki feared that when the pressure was on, he simply wouldn't back her.

Harlan glanced back over his brief sheet. "Understood, sir. Zayda Voshkie it is."

Nikki frowned. "You got to be kidding me. A bank executive tortured for an active SWIFT Network code, and that's not worth looking into?"

"The director said we're working the Voshkie case, so were working the Voshkie case," Harlan reiterated. "What part of that don't you understand?"

"Don't we at least have a responsibility to check things out?"

Harlan ignored her plea and continued to read.

"Sir," she protested.

"The decision is final, Agent Frank."

Nikki slapped her hand against the table. "No, sir, it's not."

Both men looked up, startled. Nikki took a deep breath and composed herself. She focused in on Director Kepler, adjusting her body posture to mirror his. It was a basic neuro-linguistic programming technique to help establish rapport, once taught to her by an FBI behavioral analyst. Next, she matched his breathing rate then observed him for anything of personal importance.

A large collegiate championship ring of some sort caught her attention. "What sport did you play, sir?" she asked, changing the subject.

"Basketball, Division II." He ran his finger across several of the diamonds surrounding the central stone. "Southern Indiana, Screaming Eagles," he bragged.

"Impressive."

"Thank you."

"Let's take a look at this thing from another angle, sir, if you don't mind."

Director Kepler's face tightened up. "Go ahead. I'm listening."

Nikki leaned forward. "The Cordoza crew approached us first, not the Secret Service or Homeland Security. Therefore, our operation would have tactical command that would supersede their jurisdictional charge."

Harlan smirked. "Nicole's got a point. Since we're the agency at the principal point of discovery, with an agent already in play, they'd be hard-pressed to take the reins from us on jurisdiction alone."

"True," Director Kepler replied, stroking his chin.

"Having worked with Spence firsthand while forging this cover," Nikki pointed out, "I know he's the creative criminal mind behind Cordoza's operation. If he's intelligent enough to come up with the concept, he's intelligent enough to solve the problem he's asked me to help him with. It's only a matter of time, sir."

"I don't know…perhaps. Seems like a wild goose chase here, a band of small-time white collar criminals who might have created a digital ATM in cyberspace. Do we really want to waste our time and resources pursuing this?"

"Picture this," Nikki continued. "Spence develops a working prototype that exploits ACH in some way. Criminal enterprises by the dozen line up to do business with Cordoza, who becomes insanely wealthy overnight—all because he has the sole capability to move cash in excess of ten grand, undetected, using the nation's primary financial network."

Director Kepler clenched his teeth then shook his head.

"Sir, the existence of such a prototype," Harlan reasoned, "could deal a crippling blow to the country's financial surveillance powers. It could single-handedly disable the effectiveness of the

Patriot Act, the Banking Secrecy Act, and anti-money-laundering programs. The list—"

"Is endless," Director Kepler cut in. "I know. Terrorist organizations, fringe groups, opportunist, radicals of every sort—all could be fully funded overnight."

Nikki made a sweeping gesture with her hands. "In a New York minute."

"That's not funny, Agent Frank," the director reprimanded.

"No, sir, but it's entirely plausible." She shifted position in her seat. "You look like a man of ambition. I assume a promotion to a deputy director post is in the foreseeable future."

Director Kepler smiled slightly. "Yes, that's something I aspire to achieve."

"Imagine the reaction your peers will have when they learn you had an opportunity to intervene in this matter but didn't. Do you really want to be known as someone who's afraid to drive to the basket when the ball's in the frontcourt?"

The director's face grew red. "Absolutely not."

"I rest my case."

Director Kepler stood. "Okay, Agent Frank, you have seventy-two hours to assess whether the threat is credible."

Nikki smiled. "Understood, sir."

"After that, I'm pulling the plug." The director removed a cell phone from his hip and headed toward the door. "Harlan…"

"Yes, sir?"

"Finish up with the prison-release debrief."

"Of course." Harlan fumbled with the paperwork before him. "Will you be returning here, sir?"

"Probably not. If we're going to do this, I need to get in contact with the powers that be so I can start running interference. Once Homeland Security and Secret Service step in, we'll need all the allies we can muster just to keep the ball in our court."

"Isn't that the truth," Harlan muttered.

"Meet me at the car once you're finished."

"All right, sir."

The director opened the door and walked out. Harlan turned toward Nikki. "I guess we'll get started then."

Nikki gave him a half smile.

Harlan stood and removed his suit jacket. He then reached under the table, picked up a medium-size storage box, and placed it in between them.

"What's that?" Nikki asked.

Harlan opened the box and pulled out a cell phone. "Tools of the trade."

Nikki recognized her old phone right away. "Wow, that thing has logged a serious amount of airtime."

Harlan dropped the phone back in the box. "Exactly, and it's outdated," he said, pulling out a more current model. "Your phone number remains the same. All your preferred settings, contacts, and their numbers have been rolled over. However, you'll have to check to make sure they're still valid."

"Great."

Harlan slid the phone over to Nikki, along with a black wristlet purse. "There's a state driver's license and credit card inside, along with the phone's manual. You'll have to read up on the more advanced features later. Right now we need to review our switchboard and call-in procedures."

Nikki tinkered around with the phone while Harlan watched. "Ready when you are," she said.

"Okay, call-in procedures basically remain the same. You call the lifeline, identify yourself, and leave whatever message you wish to relay to me. The switchboard will be fronting as a local beauty salon. Anyone who manages to get a hold of your phone and call the number will get a salon attendant asking when they'd like to book their next appointment. Got it?"

"Got it," Nikki repeated.

"Good. Now place your phone on speaker, dial the lifeline, and let's set up your codes."

Nikki made the adjustment and hit "1" on the speed dial. The phone rang several times before the call was answered. "Touch of Style Salon. How may I help you?"

"Agent 2294," Nikki rattled off. "Day code, business section, August twenty-sixth, identification procedure."

"Proceed."

Nikki recalled the words she had circled in the paper earlier that day. "Starbucks, employment, private sector."

"Confirmed. Hello, Nicole."

Nikki made a strange face, not expecting to be personally greeted. "Hello."

"My name's Janice," the operator stated. "I'll be assigned to you for the duration of this investigation. My cover for this assignment will be as your cousin, a beauty salon owner. We get together a couple times during the week, eat out, and talk about how our lives are going. Get the picture?"

"Yeah."

"Great. Now, checking in once every forty-eight hours is mandatory. Any messages you need to relay to Harlan, I'll pass along. In situations where you're in mixed company or can't speak freely, the following code words can be used to communicate the current situation to me clearly: *breakfast, lunch, dinner,* or *rain check.*"

Nikki repeated the words.

"*Breakfast* means emergency; *lunch*: you need the situation handled right away; *dinner*: keep a low profile and conduct surveillance; and finally, *rain check*: shut down the operation and pull the agent out."

"Understood," Nikki replied.

"Now use the code word *dinner* for me in a sentence."

Nikki thought about it for a moment. "I'm heading down to

the marina to meet some business associates. I won't be able to meet up with you for dinner."

"Outstanding," Janice said. "From there, I'd dispatch a surveillance team to tail you down to the marina and assess the situation. We're finished here, as far as I'm concerned. Is there anything else?"

"Not at this time. Thanks for the overview."

"You're welcome, Nicole."

Harlan reached back into the box and removed a Glock 27 subcompact pistol. He placed the weapon on the table—pointed toward him—then eased it over to Nikki. Her eyes widened. "What's this?"

"You're gonna need it."

Nikki stared at the handgun. "My life depends on my ability to convince people I am who I say I am, not on what I'm packing."

"Perhaps, but this is still a good idea."

Nikki slid the weapon back to Harlan. "If I have to use this, I've failed miserably. You know I like the freedom of not being strapped. It works better that way."

Harlan grabbed her hand and pushed it back in the opposite direction. "I want you to be strapped. It's important, Nicole."

Nikki withdrew, pulling the Glock toward her. "If you insist." She picked up the handgun, pointed it safely away from Harlan, and released the magazine. With her free hand, she racked the slide back then checked the chamber for a round. "Clear," she announced, before sending the slide home and returning the weapon to its original condition. She reinserted the magazine and placed the Glock back on the table.

"Nice to see prison hasn't diminished your gun skills," Harlan said with a grin. He placed a pen and several documents before her. "I need you to sign these chain-of-custody forms for all this equipment."

Nikki grabbed the pen and signed each of the forms. "Harlan, I need your help with a problem."

"What is it?"

"Well, actually, it's a pair of problems," she admitted, sliding the forms back to him.

"Go on."

"Have you heard of the Hernandez Act?"

Harlan picked up the forms and glanced over them to ensure they were signed and dated properly. "If I'm not mistaken, it's state legislation regarding the safe operation of special-care facilities. Why?"

"I went to visit my brother today."

"Oh, dear, your brother," Harlan echoed. "And let me guess... you met with some resistance."

Nikki nodded. "The facility director said I'd have to fill out some forms and submit a packet in order to receive visitation rights. That can't be right."

Harlan placed the documents back inside the storage box. "It's the law."

"She said the process could take several months," Nikki complained. "I can't wait that long. Besides, I'm the only immediate family Marty has. Surely something can be done."

Harlan shook his head. "Nope. I'm sorry, Nicole."

"Come on, Harlan. It's the least you can do."

Harlan frowned as he wiggled the side of his glasses. "You're a federal agent under deep cover; this isn't an agency concern."

Nikki crossed her arms. *Not an agency concern. Man, you've changed.*

"I know what you want," Harlan confessed. "You want me to waltz on down to the state capital, flash a federal badge, and make this all go away."

A taut grin crossed Nikki's face. *Exactly.*

"Not gonna happen. To the world, you're Nikki Frank,

seasoned criminal, and as such, you're just going to have to work within the framework of your cover. Next issue."

Nikki rubbed the back of her neck. "The warden at Shaw."

"What about him?"

"He has a penchant for viewing naked women on the job, among other things. A real sexual deviant."

Harlan raised his eyebrows. "Really? That's a pretty serious allegation."

"I know, but it doesn't change the fact that twice a month, on a Friday evening leading into the weekend shift, several women are siphoned off from the main shower detail and redirected to a private holding facility nearby. All under the guise of routine hygiene inspections." Nikki glanced down at the floor. "Several minutes later, the warden shows up, walks up and down the line, comments on each inmate's physical attributes and what he'd like to do to them, then disappears."

Nikki looked up. Their eyes met and held.

"When this first started, he'd just look around and make comments," she continued. "A few months later, it escalated to indecent exposure, followed by some fondling of a few select inmates. By year's end, he was publicly masturbating and inviting other prison employees to join in on the routine. Makes me want to delouse myself with industrial-strength chemicals every time I think about it."

"You weren't—"

"No, dear God, no…"

Harlan grabbed a memo pad and started writing. "Good."

"I do suspect some of the women were sexually assaulted, though," she added. "The new girls for sure. If you were a fresh fish and a looker, you automatically got placed on the hygiene detail. Those girls were immediately separated from our group and sent to a private room for their initial 'checkup.' I can only imagine what went on behind those doors. I've heard the stories, but hearing about it is one thing—surviving it is another."

"Cesspool," Harlan mumbled. "It's more than likely that multiple maggots are feeding here."

"You're probably right. This has been going on for years." She shook her head. "At least as long as I was there."

Harlan looked up from the pad. "What's the guy's name?"

"Penton…Warden HR Penton and Troy Castillo, captain of the guard. They're the ringleaders."

Harlan wrote down the information. "I'll get in touch with the Department of Justice tomorrow and request that a formal investigation be launched."

"Also," Nikki prompted, "have the investigation team focus their efforts on cellblock eight. That's where a good portion of new inmates are housed. They've endured a disproportionate amount of the warden's time and attention."

"Will do. In the meantime, I want you to set yourself up for an appointment to talk to the task-force psychiatrist."

Nikki closed her eyes and took a deep breath. "I'm okay… honest."

"That's an order, not a request, Nicole."

She tensed up at the command. "Fine."

Harlan reached into the storage box a final time and removed a flip key for an upscale sedan.

Nikki beamed with delight. "Is that…"

"A vehicle?" Harlan said, handing it over. "Yes."

Nikki stared at the tri-shield logo etched on the device. *I haven't driven in years,* she thought. *This ought to be fun.*

"Fully serviced, freshly waxed, and ready to go."

Nikki placed the Glock inside her purse, grabbed her cell phone, and stood. "Thank you, Harlan…for everything."

"She's parked on the opposite side of the building from where you came in," he said. "Follow me."

They left the makeshift office, walked across the warehouse, and passed through the main entrance. Parked at the far end of the empty lot was a Buick Regal Turbo: Summit White with light neutral interior and cocoa accents. Above the sculpted bumper a Georgia vanity plate read, "SOLO ACT."

Nikki sized up the vehicle. "Nice car," she noted.

"Belonged to a pencil pusher over at the Environmental and Natural Resources Division," Harlan said.

"Someone who owed you a favor, no doubt?"

He placed his hands in his pockets and glanced at his feet. "Something like that."

"Mm-hmm," Nikki said. "Now that's the Harlan I knew and loved."

The seasoned field supervisor looked over at his charge, confused. "Huh?"

"This 'corporate guy' facade thing you got going on here," Nikki said. "Suit and tie, wing-tip shoes, upscale glasses. It's not you."

"That obvious?"

"Yeah." Nikki's face slowly cracked into a gentle, disarming smile. "Wanna tell me what's going on?"

Harlan ran his hand through his hair then massaged his forehead. "I'm up for review."

Immediate recognition dawned across Nikki's face. "And you've been passed over twice already for promotion."

Harlan nodded. "Failure to advance this time mandates automatic retirement."

Nikki didn't respond right away. Her eyes darted from side to side as she processed what she'd just heard.

"I've given up everything for this job," Harlan continued. "including two wives and a condo on the beach, and now I face the possibility of ending up with nothing."

"I'm sorry to hear that," she offered in a calm voice. "But the car is still too nice."

"You're absolutely right." Harlan held out his hand. "Enough about me. Key, please."

Nikki handed it over to him and watched as he walked over to the Regal and began scratching the sedan's paint job. A momentary expression of confusion twisted across her face. "Harlan!" Nikki called out. He paid no attention to her and continued down the entire length of the drivers' side and back up over on the passengers' side.

Without a word, Harlan stopped at the trunk and removed the tire iron. Nikki's expression slid from stunned to alarmed. *Now you've completely lost it.* Harlan reared back and swung the steel lever hard, connecting with the driver's-side body panel. An explosion of steel colliding with steel left a volleyball-size dent in the vehicle. "This is crazy!" Nikki said. Harlan swung again, hitting the exact same spot. This time, the tire iron dug deep down through the white paint, exposing bare metal. He continued to strike along the body panel a third and fourth time, careful not to hit anything that would make the car unroadworthy. It was only after he pounded the other side of the Buick that Nikki realized he was enjoying himself. "That's enough," she shouted. "Stop it!"

Harlan froze. He was breathing hard and sweating profusely. When he finally caught his breath, he calmly walked back over to Nikki.

Her mouth hung open. "I can't believe you just did that," she said.

Harlan dropped the tire iron in his hand, loosened his tie, then unfasten the cuff buttons on his shirt. "And I can't believe how great that felt. Amazing."

"What about the Environmental and Natural Resources Division?" Nikki asked.

Harlan rolled his shirt cuffs up to his forearms to cool off. "Operational security."

Nikki chuckled. "Oh, that again."

"The car was too nice," Harlan reminded. "You said so yourself."

"Yeah, but vehicular vandalism isn't what I had in mind."

Harlan held his hands up and stared at his heated palms. "That was improvisational on my part. Besides, no one will wonder about this car now."

A troubled look washed over Nikki's face. "And the DOJ?"

Harlan smiled. "With General Motors providing a consistent flow of fleet cars to the government until they repay the billions they borrowed in bailout money, I don't think anyone will be too concerned over one banged-up Buick belonging to some obscure department—not with the constant influx of new vehicles readily available."

"If you say so," Nikki said, shrugging. "I'm not exactly in the loop here."

Harlan reached in his pocket and handed the key back to Nikki. "Go on. Check it out."

"After the mayhem and destruction I just witnessed, I'm almost afraid to."

Harlan snickered. "Go on."

Curious, Nikki walked over to the car and surveyed the damage: Large patches of exposed metal in a variety of warped and fragmented patterns ran the length of the sedan and stood out against the once-pristine, manufactured paint job. "If unsightly is what you were aiming for," Nikki said, "congratulations, Harlan. You overachieved."

Nikki hit the unlock button on the flip key and opened the door. It made a slight creaking sound as she got behind the wheel. Her body sunk deep into the cushioned bucket seat. A second later, she activated the interactive touch-screen stereo then started up the sedan.

The two-liter turbocharged engine sparked to life. Nikki put on her seat belt then eased the power window down. "Seems to be operating fine," she told Harlan. "I'll be in touch soon."

She backed the dented Regal out of the parking lot and headed down the winding road toward the interstate. Shifting into high gear manually, she accelerated up the ramp. The speedometer easily climbed to seventy miles an hour as she shot down the right-hand lane. The opening chords to Hall and Oates's "Out of Touch" played on the radio, the beat synchronizing with the LED display on the center console.

Nikki grabbed her cell phone and placed a call.

A male voice answered on the first ring. "Hello."

"Gem?"

"Yes."

"It's Nikki. I'm in."

CHAPTER EIGHT

Victor stepped out of the shower and put on a fresh designer suit brought up to his room by the hotel concierge. Although Lacey had left late last night, the scent of her sweet perfume and a lasting memory of her sexual repertoire still lingered.

He reflected on the way she had skillfully extracted his guarded secret, which had forced him to consider the possible repercussions of his actions. Cartel lieutenants were on a demanding career track: lots of people pushing, shoving; everybody feeling pressure, looking for the other guy to screw up. Double-dealing was a quick way to guarantee that you got dropped into a watery grave just off the coast.

Quinn had once said that if anyone in his inner circle ever betrayed him, they'd end up as shark food in the Atlantic. "Fuck up," he'd warned Victor on the day of his promotion, "and you'll get tossed into the deep. Once a year we'll sail by on the yacht, and somebody will say, 'Hey, isn't this the spot where we let ol' Vic go?' We'll pause, pour out a little champagne, and cruise on by. *Comprende?*"

If anyone else besides Quinn had made the threat, Victor would've dismissed it as melodramatic. Quinn, however, always delivered on his word, which troubled him. Victor had seen it several times over the past decade, the most memorable incident being the execution of Cesar Silva, an up-and-coming smuggler turned government informant.

When Silva had been exposed as a snitch, Quinn had placed a tire filled with gasoline around him, lit a cigar, and calmly watched as his body went up in flames. The agonizing screams and smell of burned flesh had driven Victor away from the scene. Quinn merely laughed, his roaring expression of perverse pleasure echoing into the night. It was something Victor had never forgotten. His recurring nightmares were essentially the same: a rubber tire forced around his chest, Quinn setting it on fire, and then waking up moments before burning to death. To counteract these images, Victor often relied on pharmaceutical sleep aids and an active night life.

Victor recounted the remaining cash and made a mental note of what he'd already spent. Aware of the exact amount, he stuffed the bundles inside his jacket. Finally, he grabbed his Beretta off the nightstand then left the room.

He took the elevator down to the parking garage. For several minutes, he searched for his Mercedes before finding it nestled between a Prius and an Audi.

He unlocked the silver Roadster, got inside, and started it up. While the engine was running, he entered "Paris Oaks Assisted Living Facility" into the GPS navigation panel. A few seconds later, an automated female voice announced that his route had been calculated.

Victor shifted into gear and headed for the center. Following the navigation system's directions, he cruised his way through the morning commuter traffic until he arrived at his destination forty minutes later. He parked his Mercedes in a visitor's space, got out, and headed into the main office.

The lobby was full of residents waiting to try on soccer

uniforms. Several staff members stood in the hallway behind the front-desk workstation, sorting through boxes of jerseys.

Victor approached the front desk and made a quick assessment of the receptionist behind it: redhead, midtwenties, five foot seven, no ring, no bra.

"Good morning. Welcome to Paris Oaks Assisted Living Facility," she greeted him.

"Thank you, sweetie."

She flashed a broad smile. "How can I help you, sir?"

"Oh, I could think of a number of ways," Victor replied, "in which you could be most, mmm, accommodating."

The receptionist's smile quickly faded.

"But as for today...right now," Victor said, "I'm here to make a charitable contribution."

"Great," she said, her expression flat. "Let me get you started with the paperwork."

Victor nodded. *Great. Paperwork.*

She opened the bottom drawer of her workstation, grabbed a form, and attached it to a clipboard. "These guys here could really use the funding. There's an upcoming regional qualification tournament this week for the Special Olympics. The soccer uniforms haven't been paid for. There's also transportation and equipment costs and of course staff compensation."

Victor zoned in and out of what she was saying.

"If we take regionals," she reasoned, "that's even more money: transportation to the state capital and back, food and lodging, additional clothing for the opening and closing ceremonies. The list goes on."

Victor grunted out his impatience. "What sport did you say this was again?"

"Umm, soccer," the receptionist replied, shaking her head for emphasis. "Hello?"

"I'm sorry...I was distracted by all this activity."

She handed Victor the clipboard. "May I ask who referred us to you?"

He ignored the question, his attention focused on the other end of the hall, on the petite brunette wearing a coral-pink scrub top and tight jeans. She was kneeling in front of a middle-aged male resident, shaking her finger.

"Hello," the receptionist called out again. "How'd you hear about us?"

Victor directed his attention back to her. "My boss."

"Well, good for him. An employer with his pulse on the community is always a good thing to have."

Victor gave her a sarcastic smile then glanced over the contribution form. A gut-wrenching scream from the other end of the hall startled him. He looked up. The resident standing in front of the kneeling staff member had burst into a tantrum.

Victor set the clipboard down and rushed toward the commotion. The man's repetitive chant of the word *No* grew louder. "What's going on here?" Victor asked.

"Marty's refusing to try on his jersey," replied the brunette, not bothering to look up.

"Oh."

The staff worker handed Marty the shirt once again. He grabbed it, yelled "Neeka," and hurled it across the hall.

"Nee who?" Victor repeated.

Marty screamed again.

"His sister, Nicole," the brunette said. "Ever since he saw her on the premises the other day, he's been acting out."

Victor shrugged. "So let him see his sister."

The employee stood and turned to face him. "It's comp—"

"Emma," Victor cut in. "I thought that was you."

Surprised, she staggered back. "Victor."

A mischievous grin flashed across his face. "It's been way too long, Emma."

"That's Ms. Daniel to you," she corrected him.

"Cute." *Using your mother's maiden name like that.*

"As much as I'd love to reminisce with you, I'm really busy, so let's do this later, okay?" Emma motioned for one of her coworkers to escort Marty to the time-out room.

"No, no, no. It doesn't work like that, honey," Victor said.

"Excuse me?"

"Quinn sent me."

Emma directed Marty toward her approaching colleague. "Let me tell you something, okay?" she said, directing her attention back to Victor. "Whatever you and my brother are into has nothing to do with me, so stop wasting my time."

"You can hate on him all you want. That's your business—I really don't care—but if he sends me down here for your birthday, it's gonna be me, you, and 1-800-FLOWERS."

"That's ridiculous."

Victor ran his fingers across the stubble on his chin. "Look, I'm just trying to do my job here, Emma."

She opened an empty side-room door and signaled for him to enter. "Does your job include constantly trying to sleep with me?" she asked, shutting the door for some privacy.

Victor laughed. "Getting you alone in a see-through negligee...nah, that'd be an added perk, one I'd see fit not to bill Quinn for."

Emma fired a grimacing look at him. "You're just an errand boy for my brother. Don't ever forget that."

"Fair enough, but there comes a time when a man steps out into his own."

"Really?" she said, twisting her lips into a wry smile. "And when's that?"

"Soon, real soon." Victor removed one of the bundled stacks of hundreds from his jacket. "You don't have to respect me, but you will honor this birthday gift, courtesy of your brother. Do you understand?"

Emma clenched her jaw. "How much this time?"

Victor showed her the money. "Five large."

"Five large. That's it?"

"Five large," he repeated, running his thumb through the bundle of bills.

"That's all? In this bleak economy?"

"It is what it is," Victor said with a shrug.

Emma tensed her brow. "Your profits really should be on the rise."

"Look, be grateful for what you're getting. Working this shitty job, it'd take you three to four months to make this kind of cash."

"Perhaps," she said, folding her arms. "But at least I'd sleep well at night."

"Now you see, that's your problem, Emma: you overburden yourself with a saddle of morality and ethics. Life is so much fuller without restraint. Besides, sleep is overrated."

"Says you."

Victor shook his head. "We could've been so good together."

"Not in this lifetime," Emma scoffed.

He chuckled. "You're right. I like my mares unencumbered. Besides, you'd never let me pull that saddle of morality and ethics off your back."

A taut grin splashed across Emma's face.

Victor offered her the money.

She refused it. "Take it to Bethany, up front."

Victor left the room and headed back toward the receptionist. He grabbed the clipboard off the workstation counter, attached the bundle of cash, and handed it to her.

Bethany's eyes grew wide. "Whoa!"

Victor smiled.

"You forgot to fill out the form," she pointed out.

"Honey, I don't do paperwork."

Victor walked out of the facility, got into his Mercedes, and sped out of the parking lot. He headed down Grand Boulevard for two miles then turned onto a less-traveled road to avoid traffic. The desolate stretch allowed him to increase his speed and take full advantage of the Roadster's 6.3-liter V8 engine. Ten minutes into his accelerated joyride, he noticed flashing blue lights in his rearview mirror.

"Shit!" he cursed to himself, and slowed down. The Ford Police Interceptor quickly closed the distance between the vehicles. Victor signaled, then pulled over on the side of the road and cut the ignition. The Interceptor followed. Victor quickly removed the Beretta from inside his jacket and shoved it under his seat. Several tense minutes passed as he waited. Finally, the officer stepped out of his cruiser and approached the Mercedes from the opposite side.

The patrolman tapped on the passenger-side window with his baton. Victor lowered the power windows. "Yes?"

"License and registration, please."

Victor forced a smile. *You gotta be kidding*, he thought. *As much as we pay the precinct in bribe money, I ought to get a pass here.*

A second officer stepped out of the Interceptor and made his way toward the driver's side.

"Here," Victor said, leaning across the passenger seat to hand the patrolman the requested items.

"What we got here, Hardy?" the second officer said.

"Not much, Sergeant." The patrolman glanced at Victor's driver's license. "Says here, Patrone, Victor Patrone."

"Okay. Mr. Patrone," the sergeant began, "I'm gonna have to ask you to step outside of the vehicle, sir."

Victor complied. *Quinn's definitely gonna hear about this.*

"Turn around and place your hands on top of the roof."

Officer Hardy walked over from the passenger side and joined them.

"My attorney will have me out of this before you boys can break for lunch, so you're wasting your time," Victor declared.

The two officers conversed with each other, ignoring his statement.

"Do you know who I am?"

The officers stopped speaking and turned to Victor. "Officer Hardy, the offender here wants to know if we know who he is."

The patrolman handed his baton to the sergeant. "You don't say."

The sergeant smiled then struck Victor across the back of his calves. He screamed in pain, the exploitation of his tibial nerves forcing his legs to collapse. Victor fell to the ground.

"We know exactly who you are," the sergeant replied.

Officer Hardy followed with a swift kick to his ribs. Victor gasped for air.

The sergeant knelt next to him. "You're the motherfucker who's blackmailing Lieutenant Bosky."

Victor moaned as he struggled to crawl away. *That would be me.*

The sergeant grabbed him by the hair and pulled his head back. "The name's Sergeant Twine, and we can play dirty too, pal."

CHAPTER NINE

Nikki and Spence worked throughout the night, reviewing the source code of his cutting-edge program. By 5:00
a.m. the next day, they were exhausted and called it quits.
Based on Nikki's analysis of the data, she had determined that the
threat was indeed credible but at least two to three months away
from completion.

Worn out, she returned to her room at the Compound, took
a quick shower, and went to bed. Around two o'clock that afternoon, she was jostled awake by the incessant ringing of her cell
phone. She snatched it off the nightstand and answered; it was
the Compound receptionist placing Nikki's requested wake-up
call.

She swung her feet to the floor and stretched, then headed
to the closet. Big Al, out of the kindness of his heart, had provided her with a complete wardrobe from his clothing and tailor shop in town. Nikki stared at the array of apparel for a while
before settling on a white short-sleeve blouse, jeans, and a fitted
taupe blazer.

After she had freshened up and gotten dressed, she headed
downstairs to meet with the others. Spence and Cordoza were
seated in the lounge just outside the main dining area. Spence
wore a crisp, long-sleeve, pastel-violet shirt, rolled to the

forearms, and a pair of black overdyed jeans. Despite his immaculate appearance, Nikki noticed his eyes looked tired.

Cordoza was dressed in a slate-blue sport coat with a multicolored shirt underneath. The kaleidoscope of soft pinks and blues complemented his slightly graying hair. He peered up from the morning paper and smiled at Nikki. His rich, dark-brown eyes met hers then dropped back down to an article he was reading. "Good afternoon," he said.

"Gem." Nikki took a seat on the circular couch across from him, next to Spence.

Spence acknowledged her presence with a nod. Nikki nodded back.

"So did you two get a lot accomplished last night?" Cordoza asked, continuing to peruse through the remnants of the paper still left on the table.

Spence and Nikki stared at each other for a moment. Finally, Nikki spoke up. "Yes."

"And your assessment?"

A waiter arrived and asked whether Nikki wanted something to eat. She quickly placed an order for two steak-and-pepper tacos, sautéed in extra virgin olive oil; a small salad; and a large iced tea. "With what Spence has got right now, your prototype could be fully operational in thirty to sixty days."

"And with you two, together, working around the clock?" Cordoza asked.

"Two to three weeks, but…"

Cordoza put down the paper and glanced at Spence, who shrugged. "I'm hearing this for the first time, just like you, boss."

Cordoza turned to Nikki for further explanation. "But what?"

"Something's missing, Gem."

"Like?"

"Like direction." The waiter returned with Nikki's drink and some creamy chicken taquitos with guacamole and salsa on the side. He placed the appetizers before her then disappeared back to the kitchen. "It just doesn't feel right. Can't place my finger on it."

"What do you mean, it doesn't feel right? You're killing me with this babble." Cordoza shifted his gaze. "Spence?"

"Clarify and quantify," Spence suggested.

Nikki picked up a taquito, drowned it in the dip, and took a bite. "Oh, this is so good."

The two men watched as she shoveled the rest of the appetizer into her mouth and reached for another one.

"Really, after several years of prison-cafeteria food…" Nikki paused to swallow. "The guacamole and salsa really explode in your mouth. It's damn near orgasmic."

Spence chuckled.

"I'll pass your compliments along to my chef," Cordoza said. "Now what about this doesn't feel right?"

Nikki wiped her mouth and continued. "Well, approximately eighty-five percent of cyber attacks are geared toward applications. This program Spence has developed focuses on the ACH Network as a whole. And that network is too heavily fortified."

"So what are you saying? This won't work?"

Nikki took a sip of her tea. "No, not at all. I'm just saying that if we redirect our efforts into exploiting a prospective bank's use of application software that works in conjunction with ACH, we would incur less resistance."

Spence nodded. "I can see that. Only a small amount of corporate capital is ever set aside for application hardening."

"I'm envisioning sort of a two-pronged attack with your program here: the originating bank and the receiving bank," Nikki explained. "If we keep the focus on local financial institutions, our cyber attacks will have a much greater chance of success."

Spence's eyes widened. "Ah, yes…we hit two banks

simultaneously, exploit the confusion, and manipulate currency amounts at will. Genius."

"Okay," Cordoza interrupted. "Before you two go all geek on me, how does this affect the original timeline you gave me?"

"It shouldn't change that much, Gem," Nikki said. "Three weeks, with us working around the clock." *I think.*

Willard popped in the lounge and informed Cordoza of an incoming phone call for him on the main line. Cordoza instructed him to patch it through to the Compound's intercom system and to remain on standby.

"Gem Cordoza speaking."

"Cordoza, my man. Ozzie here."

Spence whispered to Nikki that Ozzie was the "go-to" broker in the underground information world.

"Good to hear from you," Cordoza said. "Why are you using this line?"

"I keep getting voice mail. Check your cell."

Cordoza removed his phone from his hip and took a look. "My apologies. I cut it off so I could read the paper and speak with my team. What do you have for me?"

"A slot for you and your crew at a procurement auction to service a money-brokering contract out of New York."

Cordoza smiled. "Impressive. When and where?"

"Lennox Boulevard, central business district, 2438 Fairmeadow Plaza, within the hour," Ozzie said. "You're Delegation Charlie, and your password is 'bankroll.'"

Cordoza turned his cell phone back on and returned it back to his hip. "Taking afternoon traffic into account, I guess I'd better get moving."

"Yeah. Don't think this is something you wanna miss, man."

"Appreciate you, Ozzie."

"No problem. Just make sure you include the extra twenty-five percent we discussed earlier, along with my regular fee. It wasn't easy getting you a seat at the table."

"Understood."

Ozzie hung up. Cordoza motioned for Willard to pull the vehicle around front.

"Let's go," Cordoza told Nikki and Spence.

Nikki pushed the cocktail plate back and grabbed the business section of the paper. She glanced at the main article, committing the third word in each of the first three paragraphs to memory.

She pulled out her phone as the trio moved down the hallway toward the lobby. She purposefully lagged behind so she could carry out the agent-identification procedure without being overheard.

Spence doubled back and approached her. "What're you doing? Come on."

Nikki covered the phone with her hand. "Talking to my hair stylist."

Spence glared at her, annoyed. "Now?"

"Give me a second, and I'll be right with you."

As Spence rejoined Cordoza, Nikki removed her hand from the phone and spoke into it. "Hey, Janice. I won't be able to make dinner this evening. I'm tied up with some business at Fairmeadow Plaza."

Once she had covertly requested a surveillance team, she placed the phone on vibrate then stashed it back inside her jacket. Nikki quickened her pace and caught up with Cordoza and Spence. As the group exited the foyer, Willard pulled up in a white Yukon Denali.

"Take us to 2438 Fairmeadow Plaza," Cordoza directed.

The crew jumped into the SUV, and Willard sped off down the road. He darted in and out of traffic with the skill of a NASCAR driver, shaving a few minutes here and there off their travel time. Upon arrival, Willard pulled up to the executive-center entrance and let the group out. They rushed inside. A hulky guard halted their advance. Cordoza identified the entourage as Delegation Charlie then provided the password upon request. The guard backed off and escorted them to the videoconferencing studio.

Inside the studio, two other delegations were gathered around a U-shaped wooden conference table facing a high-definition video screen. Cordoza led Spence and Nikki to the unoccupied side of the table on the far right. Once they were seated, the video screen came to life. An image of a frosty-haired man dressed in a double-breasted, gray, chalked-stripe suit with a red foulard tie appeared on-screen.

"Good afternoon, delegates," the host greeted, his voice slightly distorted by the poor initial connection. "I'm Giovanni von Neer, proxy for Señor Francisco Vicente, and you're here at this sourcing event to bid on a contract to launder 2.5 million dollars up to one of our banks in New York. Directly in front of each of you is a microphone and buzzer. I ask that you buzz in to be recognized and speak clearly into the mike when you have the floor. With that said, let's get started."

The members of each delegation sized one another up. Delegation Alpha consisted of three members in coordinated business suits, while Delegation Bravo, dressed less formally, was made up of a single individual.

"Delegation Alpha," Giovanni called out clearly, the software connection issue having been resolved. "Who will be your spokesperson?"

The group conversed among themselves for a moment before nominating a wiry redheaded man referred to as Hunter.

"Delegation Bravo?"

"Docelli," the lone man with a high forehead and square jaw stated.

"And finally, Delegation Charlie."

Cordoza glanced at Nikki before speaking. "Ms. Frank will be our representative."

"What?" Nikki whispered, shocked. "Gem, are you sure?" *I have zero experience with auctions.*

Cordoza gave her an approving nod. Nervousness immediately settled in the pit of her stomach, along with the realization of the importance of this event to the crew. *I have to win,* she thought. *This is way too important.*

Giovanni gestured toward the nominees. "So we have Mr. Hunter, Mr. Docelli, and Ms. Frank," he said. "Is that correct?"

The delegations confirmed their selections with him.

"Let the bidding open up at seven days' turnover for five percent of the total amount being laundered."

Hunter hit his buzzer first. "Six days for seven percent," he proposed, with a slight Irish accent.

Giovanni repeated the bid for all to hear.

Nikki collaborated with Cordoza for a moment then pressed her button. "Five days for eight percent."

"Five for seven and a half," Docelli said, undercutting Nikki.

"Five days for seven and a half percent going once," Giovanni announced. "Going twice."

Hunter hit his buzzer once again. "Four days, ten percent."

Nikki bit her lower lip. *Damn, this is ruthless.*

"Four for nine," Docelli countered.

Giovanni repeated the most recent bid for all to hear.

Nikki leaned over and whispered into Cordoza's ear. He nodded in agreement. She buzzed in. "Three-day turnover for twelve percent of the take."

"Three days for twelve percent going once," Giovanni stated. "Going twice."

Docelli flashed Nikki a crooked smile. "Three for ten."

She returned his expression with the exact same spirit it had been given.

Hunter interrupted their nonverbal exchange with a bid for one percent lower than what Docelli had offered.

"The bid now stands at three days' turnover in exchange for nine percent of the total revenue."

The room fell silent. Nikki's phone vibrated, signifying an incoming call. She ignored it.

"Going once," Giovanni announced.

Nikki looked at Cordoza for direction. He waved her off with a cutthroat hand motion.

"Going twice."

"I'm out," Docelli declared.

"Congratulations, Mr. Hunter. I believe we have a—"

"Wait!" Nikki scrambled to her feet. "Two days, fifteen percent."

Cordoza looked shocked.

"Impossible," Hunter protested. "To move that kind of money and make it appear legit, you need a minimum of three days: two days to funnel the cash from source A to source B and a final day just to deal with the Patriot Act, Banking Secrecy Act, and a host of other financial regulations. Anything less than three days is shoddy work at best and puts everyone at risk of discovery."

"Ms. Frank, is this your final counter offer?" Giovanni asked.

Nikki's phone vibrated again. "It is, sir," she said, taking her seat again.

"All right then, Mr. Hunter has brought up a valid point. How do you address this concern?"

Nikki raised the corners of her mouth in a devilish smirk. "By taking the banking regulations off the table."

"And just how do you propose to do that?"

"I'm a bit curious about that myself," Hunter added.

Nikki pulled the microphone closer to her. "My colleagues and I have developed a program that—"

Cordoza jabbed her in the ribs.

"Ouch!" Nikki placed her hand over the mike and turned to face him. "What?"

"This isn't the time or place to discuss this," he warned her.

If not now, then when? Nikki removed her hand from the mike and continued. "As I was saying, we've developed a program that allows us to circumvent the universal anti-laundering tenet of not making any transactions larger than ten thousand dollars at any one time."

"You have my full attention, Ms. Frank," Giovanni said. "Go on."

"With banking regulations off the table, we can move larger amounts of cash over shorter periods of time, with minimal risk of exposure." Her phone vibrated one final time. "Of course, in order for us to employ this technology on your behalf, Mr. von Neer, we'll have to insist on fifteen percent."

"Wait just a minute," Hunter cut in. "Before we start chiseling side deals here, allow me to point out one thing to our host."

"And what's that, Mr. Hunter?" Giovanni asked.

"That this is nothing more than pure fantasy, conjecture, to gain your trust and your business."

"Perhaps. Go on."

"Think about it...who are these guys? Just a last-minute substitution for a group of no-shows. My colleagues and I have handled a tremendous amount of Francisco's business over the years, and I've never heard of them. What we have here," he concluded with a snicker, "is a bunch of junior-varsity players trying to get on the varsity team."

Hunter's associates laughed at his remark.

"If there is such a program," Hunter continued, "why haven't I heard of it? I've been doing this a long time now and have a vast underground network. I haven't heard a peep about such a program."

"Ms. Frank?" Giovanni prodded.

Nikki glared at Hunter. "You haven't heard of it because we just recently developed it." *Idiot.*

"Mmm-hmm, courtesy of Rumpelstiltskin, I suppose." Hunter's colleagues laughed again.

Giovanni ignored the snide remark. "And you have a working prototype, Ms. Frank?"

"Yes sir," she said confidently.

"Hmm. We'll have to take all this into consideration before making a final decision."

The delegates stared at one another, wondering how everything would play out.

"To recap before we dismiss here," Giovanni continued, "I have two offers on the table. The first one, from Mr. Hunter, is three days' turnover for nine percent of the total revenue, and the second one, from Ms. Frank, is two days' turnover for fifteen percent. Is this correct?"

The delegates confirmed their offers.

"All right. I have each delegation's contact information. I'll be in touch once a decision has been reached."

The video screen went blank. Hunter looked over at Nikki. "You'll need an awful lot of pixie dust to move 2.5 mil in forty-eight hours," he said, sneering. "Better let Tinker Bell know you'll need backup." The room burst into laughter, even from Spence. Nikki stood up and pulled out her phone. "Don't you know? I have her on speed dial," she replied, glancing down at the unrecognizable number from the missed call.

Hunter cracked a half smile at the witty remark. "Yes, of course you do."

The delegates stood then filed out of the studio, chatting.

Willard pulled around the front of the executive-center in the

Denali and picked up the crew. The ride back to the Compound was silent, except for the radio in the background. Adding to the tension was the fact that they didn't know whether or not the contract would be awarded to them.

Nikki felt Cordoza's piercing glare directed straight at her. Eventually Spence attempted to diffuse the situation by making small talk, but to no avail. Half a mile from the Compound, Cordoza finally spoke up. "I waved you off not once but twice, and you continued to push forward."

"I'm sorry, Gem," Nikki said, crossing her arms. "I thought the objective here was to win."

"Win, yes, but only under conditions favorable to us. Two-day delivery? We can't make that."

"Francisco doesn't know that."

Cordoza pointed at Nikki. "You, yourself, said it would be a minimum of three weeks before Spence's program is fully operational. What happens if we're awarded a contract but can't deliver?"

"We'll figure it out." *I hope.*

"I'll tell you what happens," Cordoza said. "Francisco's people come looking for us. At best they just take their money and shop another deal around for someone who can deliver."

Nikki raised her eyebrows. "And at worse?"

"The Lascano cartel makes examples out of all of us and puts the word out on the street about what not to do."

"Then I guess if we're chosen, we'd better deliver."

"Damn you, Nikki," Cordoza said, clenching his hands into fists. "I appreciate everything you've done for me in the past, but you're playing fast and loose, and I don't like it."

The Denali approached the Compound's gated driveway. The groundskeeper recognized Willard and buzzed him in. As he waited for the sensors to activate, a red Porsche pulled up behind them. The automated gate retracted into its frame then came to a complete stop. The vehicles entered the Compound and headed toward the hotel. Willard pulled up in front of the portico, and everyone got out. Nikki's phone vibrated again. She walked a few yards out of the way and answered it. "Hello."

"Ms. Frank?"

"Yes."

"Ms. Daniel from Paris Oaks."

Nikki watched as Cordoza headed toward the Porsche and greeted Lacey. "Oh, how'd you get this number?"

"I was rummaging through some old admissions documentation on your brother, and your information was listed. I hope you don't mind."

"Not at all. Is something wrong?"

"Oh, no. I didn't mean to give you that impression. I just called to inform you about the upcoming Special Olympics pretrials."

Nikki tucked her hair behind her ear. "Oh, that's right. During my visit you mentioned Marty and some of the other residents were training."

"This year he'll be participating in the individual skills competition for soccer."

"That's great." *Wish I could go*, Nikki thought.

"I know that officially you can't be there until you get matters resolved with the state, but if you were to be at a certain park, at a certain time, who's to say you couldn't witness your brother's participation in the event?"

Nikki smiled at what Ms. Daniel was suggesting and played along. "As long as I remain in the distance of course."

"Of course."

The two ladies laughed softly, and then Ms. Daniel provided the information.

"Thank you, Ms. Daniel."

"Please call me Emma."

CHAPTER TEN

Victor awoke to find himself lying on the ground near the passenger side of his Mercedes. He had been dragged over there, he assumed, to hide his presence from oncoming traffic. His head throbbed. As he rolled onto his side, he noticed the front tires of his Roadster had been slashed. He cursed to himself then attempted to stand. The pain in his body intensified, and he collapsed. He tried again, struggling to remain upright. Bracing himself against the Mercedes, he pulled out his cell phone and dialed roadside assistance. It was an hour before they arrived. Another two had passed before the repairs were completed and he was back on the road. Victor called to inform Quinn of his delay. It was nightfall before he arrived onboard the yacht.

He hobbled up the glass flight of stairs toward Quinn's office in the saloon, then tapped on the propped open door as a courtesy.

"Enter," Quinn announced.

As Victor limped into the room, Quinn glanced in his direction. The contusions and abrasions on Victor's face made him do a double take. "What the hell happened to you?"

"A run-in gone bad," Victor replied.

"Southside Locos?"

"Nah, personal beef."

Quinn stared, stunned. Several shoe prints on Victor's ripped jacket and trousers held his attention.

"I underestimated the situation," Victor admitted. *Gravely.*

"Obviously. Now take a seat before you bleed all over my carpet." Quinn motioned for him to step away from his desk.

Victor complied.

"So somebody's significant other finally wised up and decided to whip your—" The phone on Quinn's desk rang, interrupting him. "You chase too many skirts, Patrone."

Victor smiled halfheartedly. *I am who I am.*

The phone rang again; Quinn answered it. He gave several short replies then picked up a pen and wrote something down. "Listen up," he said, placing the phone back in its cradle. "That was Francisco. He's decided on a group to launder our proceeds from last quarter once we've made all the collections."

"The Hunter Financial Group," Victor said.

"No, the Cordoza crew."

"Who?"

"The Cordoza crew, operating out of…" Quinn glimpsed at his notes. "…the old luxury hotel, the Hanover."

"You gotta be kidding me. New blood?"

Quinn nodded.

Victor leaned forward to massage his left shoulder and ease some of the pain. "We're undergoing an organization-wide audit, and the big boss switches launderers at the last minute, and that's okay with you?"

Quinn nodded again.

"Well, it's not with me. I say we sideline the new crew and move forward with the regulars as usual."

Quinn cocked an eyebrow.

Victor sensed his apprehension. "Nobody has to know."

"I'll know," Quinn said, stroking the hair on his chin. "Stay in your lane, Patrone. Don't broadside the pecking order. And just in case you forgot, that's Francisco, *moi*, then you. Understand?"

Victor frowned.

"That's the way it is," Quinn said, "and that's the way it'll always be."

The two stared each other down. Victor didn't move a muscle, despite the pain torturing his body. Finally, Quinn broke the silence. "And the charitable donation to Paris Oaks? How'd that go?"

From your hand to my pocket, Victor thought.

"Well?"

Victor clenched his jaw tightly and tensed his face to prevent it from registering any emotion. "Under the circumstances," he began. "I'd say it went about as well as could be expected."

Quinn flashed a broad smile in response. Victor's heart leaped.

"Excellent. I knew I could trust you to handle that for me."

CHAPTER ELEVEN

The waiting room was well lit with incandescent bulbs. Several supersized charts of the female reproductive system were displayed prominently on the walls.

Thirty minutes had passed since Nikki had arrived at the clinic. Agitated, she sank deeper into her chair and crossed her legs. This simple adjustment did little to add to her comfort.

She looked around. Just about every seat was taken. A variety of women of different ages and ethnicities were also waiting to be seen by a health-care professional. Some were slumped against the taupe walls, mouths open, fast asleep. Others socialized with one another, while a few were engrossed in their electronic devices.

A brochure rack near the reception desk caught Nikki's attention. She stood up walked over toward it. The usual assortment of literature was displayed: domestic violence, breast self-examination, and HIV/STD awareness. Nikki grabbed one pamphlet of each and headed back to her seat.

"Nicole Frank," a nurse called from the hallway.

Nikki turned around and identified herself.

The nurse smiled. "This way, please."

Nikki followed her to an examination room in the back of the clinic on the left.

The nurse opened the door and motioned for her to enter the room. "Your physician will see you now."

Nikki walked inside. A man in a white coat was seated on a stool with his back toward her. The door eased shut. The physician spun around: it was Harlan.

Nikki's expression darkened. "Really, Harlan?" she said, looking around. "A cookie-doctor clinic?"

"Absolutely."

Nikki rolled her eyes.

"Gangsters aren't out following women to OB/GYN appointments. If they are, somebody at the local sex-crimes unit needs to be notified." Harlan propped his feet up on the stool's foot ring. "That aside, my primary responsibility is to help you maintain your cover. We've never had anyone in this deep before, especially with the golden opportunities you have laid before you."

Their eyes met and held for a moment.

"Fair enough."

Harlan stood and headed to the examination table. Nikki's eyes followed. "Up you go," he said, patting the upholstery.

She hesitated.

"Come on. Appearance is everything. If somebody stumbles in on us—"

"All right," Nikki said with a sigh. She climbed up onto the table. "Don't even think about mentioning stirrups."

Harlan removed the stethoscope hanging from around his neck and placed the tips in his ears. "No, this should suffice."

"It'd better."

He placed the round head of the scope on Nikki's chest. "Inhale."

She drew in a deep breath.

"Exhale."

Nikki breathed out.

The door crept open, and a second nurse appeared inside the metal frame. "Excuse me, Dr. Fisk," she said.

Harlan turned around. "Yes."

"I have the X-ray films you requested."

Confused, Nikki stared at the slender Asian nurse who had just spoken. The dark-eyed woman appeared to be in her midtwenties. Her plush black hair, cropped in a messy bob, exquisitely framed her round face and high-bridged nose.

"Come on in and let's get to work," Harlan said, gesturing for the woman to enter.

The nurse shut the door and handed him a large film jacket. "Ready when you are, sir."

Harlan opened it and removed several eight-by-ten glossy photographs. "Nicole…"

"Yes?"

Harlan paused for a moment to thumb through the pictures. "This is Special Agent Kameko Bolston, Electronic Crimes Task Force, Atlanta."

Special Agent Bolston stepped forward to greet Nikki.

"Secret Service has assigned her to us as our special liaison."

"I assume as a part of Director Kepler's strategy," Nikki added, "to retain operational oversight over this case."

"Affirmative." Harlan walked over toward the X-ray view box, placed the photos up in order, then turned on the device. "These were taken by our surveillance team at Fairmeadow Plaza shortly after your meeting."

Nikki shifted her body to get a better look at the images. "Great prints. Thirty-five millimeter?"

"Yep. Standard Nikon with a telescopic lens," Kameko replied.

"Mm-hmm, something no good chase team should ever be in the field without," Nikki said.

Kameko grinned at the remark.

"Recognize anyone?" Harlan prompted.

Nikki studied the photos on the view box in front of her. "Not really. I met these guys for the first time at the auction." She rubbed her chin as she pondered the images for a few moments. "The guy on the far left, the redhead—"

"What about him?" Harlan pressed.

"He questioned my ability to provide the service being offered to the host, made it very difficult to secure a clear win. He seemed to know an awful lot about financial transactions and moving cash illegally."

Harlan glanced at Kameko, who responded with a nod.

"Hunter...I believe that was the name he used. Mr. Hunter," Nikki added.

Kameko walked over toward the view box, removed the photo, and held it up in front of her. "Hunter McDermott, forty-one, naturalized citizen, originally from Ireland, graduate of University College Dublin. Number twelve on the Secret Service's top-twenty most-wanted list."

Nikki raised her eyebrows.

Kameko continued, "Very high business acumen, an expert at exploiting flexible governments and their officials, as well as establishing intricate networks of shell corporations."

"Impressive," Nikki said. "I can see why he distrusts me and the service I claim to be able to provide."

"McDermott has moved millions of dollars through various European banks and foreign companies for the last several years, undetected. We weren't even aware of his existence until a bank collapse in Monaco two years ago highlighted his connection to several well-funded private accounts that were seized by the microstate's government and later linked to a senior US government official."

Nikki swung her legs back and forth against the table slightly. "Wow."

"So you see, Agent Frank, you've unearthed quite a shady snake here."

"A snake," Harlan cut in, "that the Secret Service wouldn't mind getting their hands on."

"Touché, touché," Kameko fired back.

Harlan grinned.

"I gotta hand it to you, Fisk," Kameko said, "at first I thought this was just another hollow assignment, but you might be onto something here."

Nikki reached into her purse and removed a flash drive. "I hate to break up the spirit of interagency cooperation here, but—"

"But…" Harlan repeated.

Nikki handed the flash drive to Kameko. "I need some help."

"With?" she asked.

"This money-laundering program Cordoza's crew is working on, intended to exploit financial transactions processed through the Automated Clearing House."

Kameko glanced at the flash drive. "I see."

"I'm running out of time and sure could use some assistance here. Could you have your people analyze the source code? Somewhere we've reached a stumbling block and haven't been able to create a working prototype."

"I'll see what I can do."

"Agent Bolston," Nikki said, staring at her point-blank, "I need this to work. Everything depends on it."

Kameko nodded. "Noted."

"If you want to catch Hunter McDermott and others like him, this program is the way to go."

The agent narrowed her eyes. "What do mean?"

"Yes," Harlan said. "Please elaborate, Nicole."

Nikki pursed her lips and glanced toward the ceiling for a moment. "Cordoza's crew plans to use the existence of this program and its capabilities to squash the competition. When rival money launderers lose business on a consistent basis, they'll be forced to either use his crew as a proxy for their business or co-opt Cordoza's software as the standard method of conducting transactions."

Kameko continued to nod. A second later, a smile pulled at the corners of her mouth. "A Trojan horse."

"Exactly," Nikki replied, "but one with a long-term shelf life. I'm thinking five, maybe ten years out."

"That's not a bad idea."

"Imagine being able to pinpoint the movement of dirty money globally because we created an artificial bottleneck and digitally tagged the cash from the start."

Kameko smiled again. "I like it. I like it a lot."

"To sum it up," Harlan interrupted again, "we build it. We control it. We use it to our advantage."

Nikki shifted her position on the exam table, tearing the paper beneath her. "The only question now is whether we can pull it off."

Harlan turned to Kameko. "Unlimited government resources, a roomful of eggheads with academic pedigrees that would put most think tanks to shame. Shouldn't be a problem, right, Agent Bolston?"

Kameko held up the flash drive. "I'm on it, folks."

Wonderful," Nikki said.

Kameko headed back over to the X-ray view box, removed the rest of the photos, and placed them back inside the film jacket.

"I'll be in touch, Bolston," Harlan said.

The Secret Service liaison mumbled something under her breath, tucked the film jacket under her arm, then left the room.

Nikki hopped off the table and stood. Nobody liked pelvic exams, even if they were staged. "I take it we're finished here?" she asked.

"Hold on," Harlan said.

Nikki leaned back against the table and waited to see what he wanted.

Harlan removed a white envelope from inside his lab coat and handed it to her. "Before I forget."

"What's this?"

"Just something crazy I thought you should see."

Nikki opened the envelope; it was a bill for seventy-five dollars from a telecommunications company for a collect call placed at Paris Oaks Assisted Living Facility. "Seventy-five bucks?" she said, surprised. "Wow." Nikki frowned. "I hope you don't expect me to pay this."

Harlan pushed his glasses up the bridge of his nose. "Not at all. Just the cost of doing business in a wireless world, I guess."

Nikki handed the envelope back. "Good."

"Besides, I've already attempted to have the charges dismissed."

"And?"

"Some midlevel bureaucrat at the FCC mentioned some crap about the ubiquity of cell phones, 1996 deregulation, and the low service demand for pay phones."

Nikki snickered. She neglected to mention that the FCC, more often than not, was more complicit than regulatory. At Shaw, exorbitant phone fees were routinely charged to her and other inmates who were trying to stay in a touch with family and friends. It was a decades-old sham, run by privately owned companies, while the FCC looked the other way and lined its pockets with kickbacks doled out by telecom lobbyists.

Nikki forced a smile, pretending to take an interest in Harlan's rant.

"I guess," he continued, "in order to get anything done here, the director will have to speak straight to the FCC commissioner about this. Obviously this desk jockey doesn't know who he's dealing with here."

Nikki let out a sigh. *Can we get down to business?*

"I know...the inefficiencies of bureaucracy, right?"

"Warden Penton," Nikki said, changing the subject. "What's the latest with the DOJ and the investigation?"

"They're on top of it, however..."

Nikki raised her eyebrows.

He shook his head. "They've botched this thing from the start."

"What? How?"

"You know these cowboys at Justice. They went in with guns a' blazing, started dismissing staff, called it 'swift administrative action,' and now the pucker factor is so high over at Shaw that we can't get anybody to say anything."

Nikki crossed her arms over her chest. "Damn them!"

"It's the equivalent of using a meat cleaver instead of a scalpel during a delicate surgery. Personally, if it were me, I would have quietly gathered witnesses and statements in the background before ever moving in on the staff."

"So you're telling me the personnel are in 'cover their ass' mode, and the inmates are looking to see which way the direction of the wind is shifting to minimize blowback."

Harlan nodded. "Pretty much, which is why...I hate that it's come to this...but..."

"Spit it out," she urged.

Harlan looked away to avoid direct eye contact. "You might have to testify."

"Fine," she said. "Whatever it takes." *I want this guy.*

Harlan let out a sigh of relief. "Just so we understand each other, that testimony is to be given as Nikki Frank, criminal, not Nicole Frank, special agent."

Nikki jerked her head back, annoyed. *So much for the slam dunk. Inmate testimonies rarely result in high conviction rates.*

"Are we clear?"

She didn't respond. *I can't believe this guy is gonna walk, and I'll have a hand in helping him do it.*

Harlan pointed a finger at her. "Are we clear?"

Nikki shrugged. "Like diamonds."

"Great. I know you want this guy, but this is another one of those times when you have to put aside personal desires and focus on the team effort."

The two exchanged stares.

"I won't compromise your cover to right this wrong," Harland said, breaking eye contact first. "So this will have to be done in such a way as to guarantee that we have our cake and eat it too."

Nikki unfolded her arms. "I swear, sometimes this job makes doing the right thing impossible."

"That's the duality of clandestine activity: crossing lives."

"Here we go again, crossed-lives syndrome," Nikki said, frustrated at Harlan's lack of empathy.

"Undercover agents eventually reach a point during their investigations where their actual lives intersect with their assumed identities, for better or worse. This fluctuation between identities creates stressors that—"

"Can manifest physically, emotionally, and/or psychologically in an agent at any given time," Nikki finished for him. "I read the interagency memo on mental health and undercover operations too, you know."

"Then you know this is all part of the deal, why we insist on initial psychological screenings and annual assessments to follow—"

"Enough," she said, raising her voice. "I can't take any more bureaucratic bullshit."

Harlan made a face but said nothing.

Nikki looked straight at him. "I'm going to ask you again, Harlan. Is there anyone who can help me visit my brother without jeopardizing my cover?"

The door flew open just as she was finishing her sentence. Lacey strolled inside in a denim shirtdress, accompanied by the same nurse who had escorted Nikki in.

Nikki's mouth fell open.

Lacey looked directly at her. "I trust you're here to get sprayed and neutered," she said, just as the nurse left. "I wasn't sure, so I followed you. Sometimes the queen likes to see what the workers are up to."

Nikki's face turned paste white, a shocked expression chiseling its way to the surface. "Lacey..." she stammered.

"Sweetie, formal introductions have already been made. Now what were you saying about a cover?"

The wheels in Nikki's head frantically spun in an effort to formulate a plausible explanation.

"I was asking Dr. Fisk here how much insurance normally covers for a standard gynecological exam."

Lacey raised an eyebrow. "Oh."

"You know my situation," Nikki reminded her in a stern tone.

"Yes, yes, fresh out the kitty pen with less than two nickels to rub together. Sad."

"Ms. Frank," Harlan interrupted, moving between the two women to face her, "to answer your question, standard practice is an eighty-twenty split, with you being responsible for the twenty percent at the conclusion of the appointment."

Nikki mouthed a thank-you to him for affirming her off-the-cuff answer.

"So," Harlan continued, "your cost today, with insurance, is sixty dollars. If you don't have coverage, we have a social worker on staff available to help you file for government assistance."

"Excuse me," Lacey cut in.

Harlan spun around. "Who are you again?"

"Lacey Johnson."

Harlan reached up and adjusted his glasses. "And exactly how did you get back here?"

"I convinced the nurse I was your patient's sister," Lacey replied, shooting Nikki a look of disdain. "And that she needed emotional support for anxiety issues surrounding doctor's visits of this nature."

Harlan frowned. "That's a clear violation of Ms. Frank's right to privacy, ma'am."

"Like I care about that."

Nikki shook her head, empathizing with Harlan's predicament. "Excuse me, Dr. Fisk," she said, edging back into the conversation before it got more heated, "when you get a chance, could please look into that matter we were discussing earlier?"

Harlan nodded.

"Thanks," Nikki replied, patting him on the shoulder on her way out of the room. "I'll be in touch."

Harlan waved. "See you at your next appointment, Ms. Frank."

Nikki raced out of the clinic to the parking lot. *Unfreakin' believable. Talk about a close call.*

She jumped into the Buick, fired it up, and drove away. A half mile down Central Avenue, she stopped at a red light and scanned the area around her for a tail. A few of the other waiting drivers gawked in disbelief at her beat-up Regal, but there was no Lacey. Ignoring the fanfare, Nikki glanced at the dashboard. It was 1:00 p.m.; she was late.

Marty's soccer competition had started thirty minutes ago. When the light changed, she stepped on the gas and exploded up the on-ramp. The needle on the speedometer rose rapidly. Once she hit seventy, she maintained it for several miles then dropped down to fifty. The abrupt change in speed sent all cars within close proximity flying past her. Nikki glanced around at the surrounding traffic to see if she had flushed anyone out who might have been following her. Nothing.

She continued driving at a moderate pace, keeping her eyes fixed on the clock. As one final precaution, Nikki weaved in and out of tractor-trailer traffic, leaving little space for anyone to pursue. She followed the green destination signs until she arrived at the exit ramp for Burke Recreational Park.

She turned off the expressway and onto a remote highway then drove for another seven-mile stretch before taking a right on Ashford. Once she was on the dirt road, she picked up speed, a dust cloud kicking up behind her. She continued on for a quarter mile before braking to slow down. Nikki veered off the dirt road and looked for a place to park near the playing field. The lot was overflowing with a dozen or so team buses and vans. She made two passes before finding a narrow space next to a Durango that was badly parked.

Nikki picked up the wig she had brought along with her. She adjusted the rearview mirror, applied the cap, then slid the hairpiece onto her head. Once she had concealed her hairline, she styled the espresso-colored locks until she was satisfied that no one would recognize her. As a final precaution, she put on a pair of sunglasses. *Well, here goes nothing*, she thought.

The new Nikki Frank stepped out of the car and headed toward the park. The facility's grounds had been divided into three fifty-by-thirty-yard playing fields. The reduced size of the fields allowed players with disabilities to have more fun by increasing the amount of ball contact during games.

Nikki walked through the crowds, scanning the area. Six teams were currently engaged in play. On the field to the far right, she recognized the colors of one of them and moved in that direction. As an added precaution, she approached the field from the opposing team's side. If anyone was looking for her, they wouldn't expect to find her observing the tournament from the opponents' sideline.

Each team had a total of five players on the field and five players on the bench. The opposing team wore red jerseys, while the home team was clad in mustard yellow with black pinstripes.

Nikki glanced over at the Paris Oaks sideline and spotted Mrs. Ruiz and Emma, who sat next to each other on the bleachers behind the team bench.

A player wearing the number one was standing in line by the Gatorade cooler and caught her attention. Nikki instinctively knew it was Marty, if for no other reason than his jersey number matched the one Cam Newton had on in the picture in her brother's room.

Marty turned around with his drink in hand. He looked a little different than she remembered. His coarse black hair appeared fuller, and his cedar-brown complexion seemed to have deepened a shade. Marty's hefty frame had shrunken—not that he'd been very fat before, but now he seemed to have a more gaunt appearance. Nikki's overall impression was that her brother needed less sun and more home-cooked meals.

The referee blew his whistle. Startled, Nikki jumped a little. The players walked off the field to the sound of thunderous applause.

"What's going on?" Nikki asked the person next to her.

A paunchy middle-aged man turned to her. "Even match: zero, zero."

Nikki frowned.

"Don't worry…Fox Valley isn't completely out of this yet."

Surprised, she raised an eyebrow. "Oh?"

"Yeah, the game will transition to a shootout to determine the winner."

Nikki recalled her phone conversation with Emma. She had been reminded that Marty had been designated the team shooter for the event and that he'd be given three chances to kick a soccer ball from the penalty area toward an unattended goal to score points for the team.

The referee blew his whistle once again to resume play. Nikki's heart jumped when Marty stepped onto the field. She watched closely as he walked toward the top of the goal box to set up for his three kicks. The referee placed the ball in front of him and moved away. Marty took several giant steps backward then looked over at his coach, who stood on the sideline. He gave him a nod to proceed. Marty took off running down the field. Nikki's stomach churned as she watched. When Marty was within striking distance, he kicked the ball toward the goal. It streaked across the field, hit the near post, and bounced back toward him.

"Damn," Nikki said under breath.

The ball boy retrieved the ball and placed it back on the ground at the top of the goal box. The referee motioned for Marty to take his second kick. He stepped forward, swung his leg, and made contact with the ball. The checkered sphere soared through the air, seemingly on course for the corner of the far post. At the last second, however, the ball curved wide, missing the goal entirely. Marty buried his face in his hands and walked back to the starting point. Some of the players on the opposing sideline howled with laughter. Nikki clenched her fists. *Insensitive bastards.*

The referee blew his whistle a final time. Nikki held her breath. Marty struck the ball with his right foot. It skittered across the turf in a straight line for what seemed forever before rolling across the goal line and slamming into the back of the net. Nikki cheered, throwing her arms up in the air. *Way to go, Marty!*

The middle-aged spectator she had just spoken with moments earlier shot her a dirty look. Nikki composed herself. "Sorry...I root for everyone."

The man huffed out a loud breath.

"They train so hard year round for this one moment," she added. "I think we should all share in their success."

He didn't respond.

Nikki directed her gaze back to the field. Marty was over by the sidelines, high-fiving his teammates, while Mrs. Ruiz and Emma cheered him on from the stands.

The kicker for the opposing team walked onto the field. Nikki slipped back to her car to watch the rest of the competition from there. The shooter kicked. The ball took flight and landed in the back of the net. The crowd cheered. Tie game. Nikki buried her face in her hand and shook her head.

The ball boy hustled over to retrieve the ball from the orange plastic netting while the mop-haired rival practiced his kicking motion against the air. Nikki glanced up to see the referee place the ball down on the designated field marker. The shooter took three quick steps and shot. The ball arced wide, missing the goal completely. Nikki clapped to herself. *Come on. Do it again.*

The opponent set up for his final kick. The whistle blew. He shot. Goal.

Nikki slammed her fist on the armrest. "Damn it!"

Fox Valley 2, Paris Oaks 1.

Marty's team stared into the sky in disbelief. Marty clutched his head and paced back and forth in lament. While the other team celebrated on the field, Nikki's heart sank. She watched closely as the stands cleared.

The Paris Oaks players gathered their equipment and headed toward the team bus. They proceeded through a gauntlet of applause and cheers from Mrs. Ruiz and other staff members.

The bus pulled out of the parking lot thirty minutes later. Nikki tailed the vehicle from the recreational park to Angelo's Pizzeria, where she assumed they were going for a postgame dinner. When the bus pulled into the eatery, she pretended to be waiting to pick someone up from another establishment along the strip.

The team got off the bus and headed inside. Nikki remained in the parking lot for another fifteen minutes before venturing inside.

Once inside Angelo's, she was seated by the hostess at a table near the front door. Nikki ordered a mineral water then scanned the room. There were several rows of tables, each covered with a plastic checkered tablecloth; coordinated booths along the perimeter; and a replica brick oven nestled in the back. The place was noisy and warm. Adult contemporary music flooded through the restaurant audio system, and an interwoven smell of garlic, pepperoni, and freshly baked bread drifted from the kitchen. Nikki's stomach grumbled.

Off to the side, she noticed a semiprivate banquet room full of soccer players. Nikki fumbled with the menu as she kept an eye out for Marty. The waitress had come and gone with her drink and some appetizers when Marty broke away from the group. Nikki got up and followed him to the restroom. She pushed open the door and marched in. Marty jumped back. "This is the men's room," he said.

Nikki stared at her brother, thrilled to finally see him after so many years. Tears collected at the corners of her eyes.

"Leave," Marty insisted, pointing to the door.

She smiled but didn't move.

"Now!"

Nikki removed the wig from her head, revealing her true identity.

Marty's eyes grew big.

"It's me," she announced. *Say something.*

It took a moment for Marty to process what was going on. "Neeka!" he finally exclaimed.

"Yes, Martini."

"Neeka!"

Tears flowed freely down Nikki's cheeks. She extended her arms in his direction. Marty rushed toward her, and the two embraced. "Where you been?" he asked softly.

"Work," Nikki replied, slightly embarrassed to admit she'd prioritized her career over him. It wasn't that she didn't care. She did. It was the allure of undercover work and life out on the street that kept her away. It intoxicated her.

The two siblings pulled away from each other and held hands. Nikki couldn't stop smiling at her brother.

He smiled back. "You look tired, Neeka."

"Why do you say that?"

Marty let go of her grasp and placed his hands on his hips, akimbo fashion. "Because you always working," he chastised her. "Never see you anymore."

Nikki's smile quickly faded. "I'm sorry, Martini."

"We're family," he insisted.

She lowered her eyes to avoid his. "I know…I'll do better."

"Good. Now let's eat."

Nikki cringed at the suggestion. "I can't," she said, knowing she was already taking a big risk of being discovered by being with her brother in the men's room.

Marty's smile drooped. "Why not?"

"Some people don't want us to be together," Nikki said.

Marty patted his stomach. "Aren't you hungry?"

"Yes," she reassured him. "But we would upset a lot of people if we ate together right now."

Marty followed up with another automatic "Why?" It pierced Nikki's heart to see him working to comprehend what she had said. She grabbed his hands and squeezed them tight. "That's not important. What's important is that I can fix this."

Marty nodded, looking a little relieved.

"But you have to promise me something."

Marty's eyes lit up. "What?"

Nikki leaned forward and caressed his cheek. "That you won't tell anyone you saw me…not Ms. Daniels, not Mrs. Ruiz, not any of your friends."

Marty smiled an "okay" and followed it up with a nod.

"Understand?"

"Yeah, I understand."

Nikki held up her right hand in a fist and extended her little finger. "Pinky swear."

Marty mirrored her gesture then wrapped his finger around hers. "I swear."

"I love you," Nikki said, hugging him again.

"Love you too, Neeka. Mean it."

CHAPTER TWELVE

Victor paced the floor in his suite at the Chateau Regency. His mind was preoccupied with several thoughts: Quinn's random request for him to make a cash donation on his behalf to Paris Oaks, Bosky's use of excessive force as payback, and the excruciating pain he still felt as he moved.

The living room was occupied by three associates he'd done business with in the past: independent contractors, discreet, reliable, all "visiting" from out of town. They were far from the brawny, well-dressed, gun-toting Italian guys the term "hired muscle" often brought to mind, the obvious distinction being that the group was multiethnic.

From the Windy City, the trio often took jobs together and only referred to one another by gemstone monikers. The black gentleman was called Onyx; his Latino colleague was Topaz; and the Caucasian went by Jasper.

Victor stopped in midstep in front of the sofa and stared at the men before him. They were seated in lounge chairs around a square mahogany coffee table.

Topaz fumbled with his fingers, twisting them. "You gotta go to the bathroom or something, *ese?*"

"Bathroom, hell," Onyx cut in. "He needs a muthafucking doctor. Who fucked your face up like that, Patrone?"

"Yeah, *esé*, we here fo' that retribution?"

Victor ignored the barrage of questions. Instead, he patted himself down and checked the pockets of the new suit the concierge had delivered to him.

"Gentlemen," Jasper said, raising his voice, "enough."

Victor reached inside his jacket and pulled out the torn newspaper announcement. "There's a government auction," he began, placing the advertisement on the coffee table, "open to the general public for the next seventy-two hours."

Jasper looked at Topaz and Onyx. "And you want us...to do what?"

"Go shopping, of course."

"For what, *esé*?"

Victor smirked at Topaz, aggravating his facial injuries. "Toys for our little surprise party."

Onyx shook his head. "Who's picking up the tab for this, Patrone?"

"Don't worry—I got it covered."

"You'd better," Onyx scoffed.

Victor tossed the second five-thousand-dollar stack of cash he had in his possession onto the table.

"Now that's what I'm talking about." Onyx scooped up the bundle and ran his fingers through the bills. "Woo-hoo!"

"And the shopping list?" Jasper asked.

"Written on the currency band."

Jasper motioned for Onyx to toss him the stack of cash.

"There are three items and only three items we need," Victor said.

Jasper glanced at the plain white strap securing the bills. A numbered list written in pencil was scribbled across the band.

"Also, don't forget to pick up our package from FedEx," Victor reminded them.

Topaz held up the purple-and-orange pickup notice. "Roger, *esé.*"

Victor rolled his shoulders to alleviate some of his soreness. *Pigs worked me over real good,* he thought bitterly.

Onyx stared at him for a moment, shook his head, and frowned. "Any muthafucking thing else?"

Victor reached back into his jacket, removed the remaining bills he had left, peeled off another grand, and handed it to Jasper, along with a pair of spare key cards to the suite. "Rendezvous back here when everything's completed."

The men nodded, stood up, and left. Victor went into the bathroom and freshened up.

Twenty minutes later, there was a knock on the door. Victor peered through the peephole. It was Lacey, dressed in a leopard-print dress. He eased the door open and welcomed her in.

"Got your message," she said, entering the room.

"Good." Victor looked her over. Her body-flaunting garment exposed a generous portion of her bronzed skin while encasing her sultry curves.

Lacey spun around and adjusted her cleavage.

"Well," Victor prodded, wanting to address the obvious.

She stared at him blankly.

"The face," he finally said. "Aren't you gonna ask about it?"

"Nope."

"Why not?"

"It's not my place to do so." Lacey shifted her eyes to the left and glanced down the hallway leading toward the bedroom. "Besides, I'm here to fuck. Where's the cash?"

Victor laughed. "My, my, my, you are curt."

Lacey flashed him a halfhearted smile and held her hand out to be paid.

Victor reached into his jacket again, removed a grand, and handed it to her. "Here."

"Thank you very much," she said, warming up to him instantly.

Victor frowned. *Just like four quarters—always changing for a dollar.*

"You were saying something about your face?"

"Never mind," he said, straightening his jacket.

"Well, don't be such a sourpuss," she said. "It's the cost of doing business. What else is new?"

Victor gave Lacey a sly smile. "I'm onto something big here, cupcake."

She closed the distance between them and placed her hand on his chest, then slid it down slowly. Victor closed his eyes as her hand descended lower.

"I suspect in a few minutes I'll be onto something big too," she said, fondling him through his slacks.

Victor stiffened. "Seriously, this thing could solve all my problems."

"Mm-hmm," Lacey said, ignoring him as he went on and on about the brilliance of his idea. Working her way back up toward his torso, she leaned in close and whispered for him to be quiet. "Now how about a little taste of sin?"

Victor nodded vigorously.

Lacey smiled then gently eased her hand around the Beretta protruding from his shoulder holster. This time Victor didn't flinch; instead, he relinquished control, allowing himself to surrender to being vulnerable. "It's such a rush, just being with you," he confessed.

Lacey disengaged the holster's strap, freeing the weapon.

"Go away with me, cupcake."

Lacey stopped what she was doing and stared at Victor, stunned.

"Me and you," he emphasized. "Just poof, disappear."

"What?"

"We'll put all this behind us. Start fresh, no worries about tomorrow."

Lacey was caught off guard by the strange nature of Victor's ramblings. Her voice snagged in her throat. "That's crazy talk," she said, backing away from him. "Besides, I have a life here, a good one. Don't see much profit in running away."

Victor snapped and shoved her to the floor; Lacey screamed.

"Money-grubbing bitch," he said, grabbing her by the hair and dragging her to the door. "Get out!"

Lacey scrambled to her feet and rushed out of the suite.

Victor followed, throwing several hundred dollars at her. "Fucking whore."

Lacey scooped up the cash then rushed to the elevator.

"And don't come back!" he yelled, slamming the door closed.

CHAPTER THIRTEEN

A nother night had passed at the Compound. Nikki and Spence still hadn't made any substantial progress toward completing a working prototype of the money-laundering program. Spence, exhausted from his effort, stood first and dragged himself from the lounge to the elevators in the lobby. Nikki followed. Both were thinking the same thing: *Time to unwind.* The endless hours of keyboard pounding, analyzing code, and reconfiguring data had taken a toll on them.

When they arrived on the second floor, the two separated and headed in opposite directions. Nikki arrived at her suite first and quickly disappeared behind the door. She went straight into the bathroom, turned on the tub faucet, and poured in a generous amount of bubble bath. The room filled with steam. Moments later, the mirror had fogged, and the scent of cherry blossoms saturated the air.

Nikki undressed then stepped into the bathtub. She slid into the warm water until the suds covered her shoulders. While soaking, she grabbed the dog-tag pendant hanging from her necklace and ran her thumb and forefinger over it. An image rose in her mind of her mother chasing her naked brother around the house while he yelled, "Nature boy!" She was eight and mortified in front of a house full of guests. He was eleven. It was her first slumber party, and he was making a spectacle of himself. Her mother had promised Marty would behave, but as Nikki knew, his behavior was often unpredictable.

She giggled to herself. *Nature boy. Good one, Martini.* She rested her head against the edge of the tub and closed her eyes, dozing off. When she woke up several minutes later, the water was lukewarm. Nikki got out of the tub and dried herself off. She walked over to the dresser, slipped into a pair of pajama bottoms and a scoop-neck tank top, then crawled into bed to take a nap.

Four hours later, a knock on the door woke her up.

"Just a minute," she answered. Groggy and disoriented, she eased herself out of bed and slowly made her way to the door.

A second knock followed, much louder than the first.

Nikki frowned. "Hold on, damn it."

She opened the door just a crack and peered out. It was Spence, smiling. He was casually dressed in jeans, an oxford shirt, and a cream sport coat.

"Rise and shine, sunshine," he said.

Nikki opened the door fully. "You gotta be kidding, right? Seems like I just laid down."

"Unfortunately, no. The boss wants to see us now."

"Great," she huffed. "You know what this is about?"

Spence shrugged. "No clue."

Nikki stepped into hallway and shut the door behind her.

Spence gave her a strange look, one she couldn't quite place. "What?"

"There's something I want to show you." He reached behind his back and pulled out a Smith & Wesson semiautomatic pistol from underneath his jacket. "Check it out."

Nikki's eyes widened. "Whoa!"

Spence flashed a self-approving grin. "Sweet, isn't it?"

"What are you doing with that?" Nikki asked, shifting to move outside the line of fire.

"Personal protection. Figure if we get this deal with Francisco, I might need it—just in case things get hairy. Know what I mean?"

She shook her head. "This is a bad idea." Spence frowned. "We're brokers who specialize in white-collar crime, not lawless thugs running the streets."

Spence rolled his eyes.

"We're better than that shi—" Nikki cut herself off. "Put that thing away, and let's go see what Gem wants."

He tucked the gun back into his waistband holster, and the two proceeded toward the elevators. When the next available car heading down arrived, Spence held the door open until Nikki entered.

"Thank you," she said.

He pressed the "L" button, and the elevator gradually descended to the ground floor. Once the doors opened, he led the way toward the lounge just outside the main dining area. Cordoza and Lacey were already present, waiting on them. Lacey wore a beautiful geranium-colored, short-sleeve dress with diamond laser-cut trim. The dress hugged her figure through the bodice, right past the hips, then flared away from her body. To complete the look, she had added an antiqued-gold necklace with multicolor flower stations and a matching pair of pearly-enamel flower earrings. Cordoza stood while Lacey sat on a sectional sofa.

"If you're gonna be late, at least be properly dressed," Lacey said, commenting on Nikki's pajama bottoms and tank top.

Nikki raised her eyebrows. "Don't start with me!"

"Apparently somebody needs to. For someone who's just been released from prison, uniformity doesn't seem to be your strong suit."

Spence lowered his head and chuckled.

"Gem, does she have to be here?" Nikki asked.

Lacey's mouth dropped open. "Excuse me?"

"Ladies..." Cordoza, said, raising his voice.

The women stopped their bickering and looked over at him.

"Let's get down business. Seats, please."

Spence and Nikki joined Lacey on the sectional. Spence sat between them to act as a buffer.

Cordoza glanced at Nikki. "Late night?"

"Extremely late."

"Progress report?"

Nikki sunk deeper into the sofa's pillows. "Spence and I tweaked the program's sniffer, adding a keylogger with stealth and remote-access components. The only problem now is expanding the amount of data the keylogger can store without collapsing the entire program matrix."

A puzzled look washed over Cordoza's face.

Spence leaned forward. "Basically, we made some moderate corrections and added an enormous amount of new source statements to the program, boss."

"Thank you. And the estimated timetable?"

"A week and a half," Nikki answered, "give or take a few days."

Cordoza stepped in front of her. "That long?"

"Pretty much, Gem."

He let out a long breath. "You know that puts us in an awkward position. Thanks to you, we have potential clients under the impression that we have a workable prototype. When they find out we don't, what will that do for business?"

Lacey looked at Nikki and shook her head. "Ruin it—that's what it'll do…ruin it."

Nikki folded her arms across her chest. *Fucking bitch.*

"It won't come to that," Spence interjected.

Cordoza stepped away from the sectional. "Let's hope not, or we're all screwed."

The discussion was interrupted by the arrival of a waiter holding a serving tray covered by a silver cloche. "As you requested," he announced, handing the platter to Cordoza.

Cordoza took the tray and placed it on top of the bar. "Thanks, Max."

The waiter slipped out of the room.

Cordoza lifted the silver dome off the platter, revealing a business envelope and several stacks of bound cash. "The reason I gathered you all here together—" he began.

"Payday," Spence cut in. "Right, boss?"

"Yes."

Everyone smiled, except Lacey, who frowned. "A bit melodramatic, wouldn't you say, Gemini? The whole 'waiter, covered tray' thing?"

Cordoza gave her a mischievous grin. "Perhaps, darling, but effective nonetheless. You guys thought you were gonna eat, didn't you?"

Nikki smiled. "I could use some breakfast."

Cordoza grabbed a stack of cash off the platter and tossed it toward her. She caught it and leafed through the notes. She estimated there were fifty one-hundred dollar bills. She shook her head. *Almost a complete month of expenses here for Marty's care at Paris Oaks, and Gem tosses it around like a rapper at a strip joint. Unbelievable.*

Another stack of cash flew through the air toward Spence. He snatched it in midflight then pumped his fist. "Thanks, boss."

Cordoza picked up the last bundle and prepared to pitch it to Lacey.

She shot him a dirty look. "I'm not some dog you can play fetch with."

Cordoza clenched his jaw. "Baby, I wasn't suggesting you were."

"Good. Now come to Mama."

Cordoza walked toward her and placed the money in her hand. "Your spending allowance for the month, doll. Getcha something nice, real nice, something we both can enjoy." He gave her a knowing look.

Lacey smiled wide.

"I think I'm gonna be sick," Spence whispered to Nikki.

Nikki snickered. *You aren't the only one.*

Cordoza went back to the bar, picked up the business envelope, and handed it to Nikki. "Here you go."

She gave him a puzzled look. "What's this?"

"Part of the 'stay out of jail free' card I promised you when you came back on board with us."

Nikki tore open the envelope. Inside was a payroll check made out to her from the Myriad Conglomerate in the amount of $1,489.75 for IT consulting.

"To show your parole officer," Cordoza said.

Nikki looked up. "You don't miss a beat, do you, Gem?"

A playful grin spread across his face. "Nope."

Nikki glanced back down at the check. "You even have the signature of Carson Lancaster the third here."

Cordoza gave a slow nod.

"Will it cash?" she asked.

"Of course. Isn't that the point?"

Nikki flashed him a smile. "Impressive. Thank you."

Cordoza smiled back. "You're welcome."

Willard entered the room and approached Cordoza. "Sir, incoming call, main line."

Cordoza frowned. "Now?"

The driver nodded.

"Have the receptionist take a message."

"The caller says it's urgent."

"It usually is," Cordoza said with a sigh. "Patch it through then."

Moments later, a male voice came over the wireless intercom system. "Hello?"

"Gem speaking," Cordoza replied.

"Mr. Cordoza, my name is Victor Patrone. I've been asked to

establish contact with you on behalf of our mutual friend in New York…Excuse me, are we on speaker?"

"Yes, we are."

Victor said nothing further.

"Rest assured," Cordoza continued, "that this is a secure line, and the only people listening in on this conversation are my crew."

The soft, steady sound of the caller's breathing was broadcast over the speaker for all to hear. Concerned, Nikki looked at Spence, who shrugged.

"Is that going to be problem?" Cordoza asked, following up.

There was no response from the caller.

"Mr. Patrone, are you there?"

Silence.

"Mr. Patrone?"

Victor coughed. "I'm here."

"Excellent, I thought we lost you."

"I suppose the setup you have in place is just fine. If Francisco trusts you, who am I to judge?"

"Shall we proceed then?" Cordoza asked.

"As I was saying, our mutual friend in New York has decided to award your crew a contract to handle a large financial transaction on his behalf."

The group celebrated among themselves. "That's good news, Mr. Patrone," Cordoza said, motioning for the group to quiet down.

"I'm calling to discuss the particulars with you."

"Okay, let me turn you over to my associate, Spence Taylor. He handles planning and logistics."

Spence stood up from the sectional and walked over toward Cordoza. "Spence Taylor here," he announced.

"How are we going conduct our business going forward, Mr. Taylor?"

"Good question, Mr. Patrone. Let's start with packaging," Spence said, clasping his hands. "The money you provide us will be separated and packed by denomination…none of that party-pack bullshit."

Victor laughed. "What do you know about party packs?"

"Look, I've kicked it with my fair share of street dealers, and I know everybody's skimming from the till. Part of the problem is that you're in a cash-intensive business with little or no oversight. It's not uncommon to have twenties, fifties, and hundreds lying around in no particular order. If Ricardo needs gas money, he grabs a twenty; Jerry wants to take his ol' lady out, he picks up a hundred, and so forth and so on. Bottom line: don't bring me a suitcase full of cash with a bunch of fives, tens, and twenties thrown together to make up a million. "

Nikki gave Spence a thumbs-up.

"Understood," Victor replied.

"This will make counting and verifying the received amount less burdensome. Anything other than a bag full of cash separated by denominations, and we charge an eight-percent administrative fee for having to make the money bank-ready ourselves."

"No party packs. Next?"

"Since we've never done business together," Spence continued, "it's only reasonable to assume everybody's going to be a little skittish. To help alleviate the angst, I propose we agree to one vehicle from each party, with no excessive entourages."

"Noted."

"Finally," Spence said, tugging on his sport coat, "there's the matter of the cash-drop time and location."

"Yes, there's always that, Mr. Taylor."

"Two p.m. today, Montrose Train Station parking lot, just beyond the passenger terminal, row seventeen."

"Montrose," Victor repeated.

"Yeah, large bags and suitcases won't seem out of the ordinary there. There's minimal security, and if things get dicey, there are two major expressways within a quarter of a mile of each other."

"Sounds like you've done your homework."

"Always."

"Kudos, Mr. Taylor. Kudos."

"Mr. Patrone," Cordoza interrupted.

"Yes?"

"I believe that concludes our business together until the exchange."

The line went dead.

Nikki jumped to her feet and spoke before anyone else could. "People," she said, clapping to get their attention. Everyone looked in her direction. "Let's focus on how we're going to place this money once we receive it."

Lacey's face went blank.

Cordoza saw her confusion. "Baby, that's shop talk for putting the dirty money into the financial system or retail economy."

Lacey smiled halfheartedly. "Oh."

"We make the eight-hour run to the Gulfport," Spence suggested. "Hit up the casinos, and purchase a helluva a lot of chips, which we redeem for large checks by the end of the night. Take the checks, deposit them into a bank, and go from there."

Cordoza shook his head. "Too easy to get pinched. That might have worked in the seventies, but with the advent of multimillion-dollar surveillance equipment and entire departments dedicated to watching every little thing patrons do, we'd instantly be made. Besides, a true whale conducts business via an established line of credit, backed by a bank. Anybody showing up with a suitcase full of cash is just asking for trouble."

"What if we make use of a bank employee?" Nikki proposed. "Someone high enough on the corporate ladder to deposit the entire two and a half million?"

Spence's eyes widened. "What do you mean? Bring in an outside partner?"

"Not exactly."

Everyone kept quiet, unsure where she was going.

"I was thinking blackmail," she announced.

Spence's mouth fell open. "Really?"

"Yeah, we conduct some surveillance, find out which bank employee is most susceptible to coercion, and exploit that vulnerability to our advantage."

"Too time-consuming," Cordoza pointed out. "Besides, it's just plain messy all the way around."

Nikki sat back down on the sectional. Lacey gave her a dirty look then turned her back to her. "This seems like an awful lot of work on our part for a meager fifteen percent, Gemini."

Cordoza grinned. "Baby, it's not about percentages. It never has been."

She shot him a confused look. "Okay, what am I missing here?"

"Opportunity."

She flipped her bleached-blond hair behind her. "Opportunity for what?"

Nikki huffed at the wanton display of vanity. *Ditz.*

"To earn Francisco Vicente's future business," Cordoza replied.

"Oh."

"And to obtain access to his many contacts."

Lacey nodded slowly. "Makes sense, hon."

"Great, now that the tutorial is over," Nikki snapped, "can we get back to discussing how we're gonna place this money once we collect it?"

Spence chuckled then sat back down next to her. "How 'bout we open numerous accounts across several brokerage firms, evenly disperse the capital, and buy and sell securities?"

Nikki paused for a moment. "Interesting idea."

"Our client can't exactly tell the IRS he made several million dollars selling drugs, but he can say he purchased the right stocks, at the right time, with the right splits."

"I'm concerned," Cordoza said, crossing his arms.

"With?" Nikki asked.

"After the fallout from the Bernie Madoff fiasco, the Securities and Exchange Commission is taking a beating by the government on oversight."

Nikki looked to Spence for a response.

"Which means the anti-money-laundering programs for nearly every brokerage house in the country are on steroids," he concluded. "Enhanced identification procedures, immaculate record keeping, heavily scrutinized internal reporting systems. You name it—all the stops will be pulled out on this for quite some time."

Cordoza smiled at his protégé. "Exactly."

"Okay," Nikki said, "since we can't exactly show up at Charles Schwab with a couple of million in cash, what do we do? Any other ideas?"

Cordoza stepped toward the sectional and gestured toward Spence and Nikki. "You two, pick a bank and hack into its lodge accounts. Once we have control of several of them, we'll infuse the money into the banking system using Smurfs."

Lacey laughed out loud, disrupting the flow of conversation. "Smurfs, Gemini?"

Cordoza gave her a cursory glance. "Not the little blue cartoon characters, baby."

She screwed up her face. "Okay, then, what are you talking about?"

"I'm talking about innocuous, plain-looking folks we enlist to make deposits on our behalf, the idea being to distribute and deposit the money so that it appears not to come from a single source."

"Gotcha."

Cordoza directed his attention back to his crew.

"Taking control of a few charity accounts won't be a problem," Spence said.

"Good."

"However, the second part, well, that's kinda of iffy."

Cordoza frowned. "How so?"

"Because we'll incur a positive control deficit."

"What?"

"The larger the amount of cash that we're asked to handle, the more oversight will be required."

Cordoza shook his head. "Nikki?"

"He's right, Gem." She tilted her head to the side. "Banking regulations cap deposits at ten grand before notifying the government, which means for every hundred thousand, we need ten people to make deposits. That's two hundred fifty Smurfs total. Even under the best circumstances, we couldn't control that situation, not with just the three of us."

"Then what's the answer?" Cordoza pressed.

The discussion spiraled into silence. Nikki glanced down at the check she was holding. *Myrrh, Myrtle, Myriad.* Then it hit her. *Conglomerate.* The word leapt off the check at her. A conglomeration was a corporation consisting of a number of subsidiary companies. She jumped to her feet again. "I got it!"

Everyone looked at her, surprised.

"Gem, you said when you bought this place you went through the trouble of having a fictitious organization created, with several subordinate agencies to conceal the fact that you were the sole owner, right?"

Cordoza nodded.

"And the country of incorporation for your fictitious organization?"

"Venezuela, but how's that relevant to our current situation?"

"We get the money into the system by taking advantage of the global economy and international trade, using the Myriad Conglomerate and its subsidiaries as agents."

"Okay, now you're gonna have to do some explaining here."

Nikki took a deep breath. "It's not uncommon for corporations to do millions of dollars' worth of business worldwide. So we simply have the Myriad Conglomerate conduct a business transaction with one or two of its subordinate companies or vice versa…something basic, like an equipment purchase."

Spence grinned. "And since we have control of all the entities involved, and everything appears legitimate, we'll slip under the radar."

"Precisely," Nikki said, beaming.

"Baby, girl," Cordoza said," I love your thinking."

"Thanks. Now it would be to our advantage to ensure that whatever's purchased is hard to appraise."

"Like art," Cordoza suggested.

"Right, but I was thinking more along the lines of antiques."

"Why?"

"It just seems to fit in better with everything you already have in place, Gem. For example, one plausible scenario could be that company A, who you've contracted to help restore this place back to its early-twentieth-century appearance, subcontracts the Myriad Conglomerate to purchase antique furniture unique to the time period on its behalf."

Cordoza's face lit up. "I like it. Go on."

"Since antiques are hard to place a true value on, we simply fudge the numbers between the corporations and take advantage of the concept of product undervaluation. We say we purchased something for a hundred grand on paper but take two and a half mil as a cash payoff. After all, it is a 'historical restoration' project, right?"

Cordoza laughed. "Right."

"We draft phony invoices and receipts," Nikki continued, "maybe even go so far as to have some guys overseas send over a few shipments of stuff to keep up appearances. Bottom line: we control all the companies involved and all the accounts associated with those companies, making it relatively easy to place Francisco's money into the system."

"And once it's in the system," Spence concluded, "we use my program to digitally maneuver it through the mass array of banking security software up to New York."

Lacey turned toward Spence and gave him a stern look. "Now hold on a minute. Your program doesn't even work, and here we are planning this scheme like everything's just fine."

Spence clenched his jaw. "Like I said, I'll get it to work."

"Well, I'm not convinced you can."

"You stick to tanning and whatever it is you do with your hair and let me worry about our digital dilemmas."

"Spence," Cordoza called out, reprimanding him, "quit being so flippant."

"I wasn't—"

"Whatever," Lacey said, standing up. "I'll be out shopping." She tossed her hair back and stormed out of the room.

Nikki frowned. "Gem, we need to get in touch with the attorney who set up the Myriad Conglomerate, as well as his associates."

Cordoza pulled out his cell phone and started dialing. "Everyone, let's rendezvous back here at one."

The group dispersed. Nikki raced back to her suite and freshened up. When she finished, she rummaged through her closet to find something to wear. Ordinary wouldn't do; it had to be something sleek and oh-so tight. When it came to money drops, experience had taught her that distraction was the name of the game. Everybody would be on edge, and a healthy dose of sensuality never seemed to hurt. The more eyes she could keep focused on her "assets," the less likely things were to get out of hand.

She caught a glimpse of a slinky red dress at the back of the closet. She pulled it out, undressed, and held it up next to her body. Her attention was instantly drawn to a small fold of flabby skin visible over her stomach. Her heart quickened. *Is that belly pudge?* Nikki shook her head in disbelief. *Girl, you need to step it up. This mirror does not lie.*

She slipped the tight-fitting dress over her head and down over her hips then put on a pair of matching pumps. When she finished, she looked at her reflection again in the mirror. *Not bad.*

She made some minor adjustments then picked up her cell phone from the nightstand. She quickly accessed the Internet and pulled up a digital version of the morning paper's business section. Glancing over the main article, she identified the third word in each of the first three paragraphs and committed them to memory. When she finished, she hit "1" on the speed dial.

"Touch of Style Salon," an upbeat voice announced. "How may I help you?"

"Agent 2294," Nikki replied. "Day code, business section, identification procedure."

"Please proceed."

"Employee, retailer, shift."

There was a brief pause while the operator verified the words. Nikki took a deep breath.

"Confirmed," the operator said. "How's my favorite cousin?"

"Outstanding, and how 'bout you, Cousin Janice?"

"I can't complain, and if I did, it wouldn't do any good. What do you have for me today, Nicole?"

"Relay to Harlan that Cordoza's crew has just been awarded the brokering contract. Money exchange goes down today at fourteen hundred hours, Montrose Train Station parking lot, row seventeen."

"Noted. Anything else?"

"Surveillance only, no apprehension. I want to play this thing out."

"Okay, girl, you be careful out there."

"Will do, cuz."

CHAPTER FOURTEEN

Victor glanced at his watch; it was almost two. He'd been rushing around all morning. First, there was the transportation of Francisco's proceeds to a cartel safe house in the city. Next came the endless counting and organization of the money according to Cordoza's specifications, something Victor personally had supervised, and finally there was the matter of delivery of the two seventy-five pound duffel bags to the agreed-upon drop site.

He kept the engine to his Roadster running while he waited for someone to show up. A white Yukon Denali pulled into the train station's parking lot at exactly 2:00 p.m. and stopped several yards away from him. The tinted windows were so dark that Victor couldn't make out how many people were inside. The passenger door facing him opened. A well-groomed, fashionable-looking man stepped outside of the vehicle.

Victor reached inside his jacket, removed his Beretta, than raised it in his direction. The man lifted his hands up and approached slowly. "Spence Taylor," he announced. "You Victor Patrone?"

"I am."

"Pleased to meet you."

Victor eased himself out of the Mercedes. "Have everyone but the driver exit the SUV."

Spence turned around and motioned for Willard to lower his window. "Everyone get out except you, Wills."

The doors opened then slammed shut. Nikki and Cordoza walked around the Denali and joined Spence.

Victor zeroed in on the swaying of Nikki's hips as she strutted forward. The plunging V neck of her red dress and the natural bounce of her breasts brought a smile to his face. Victor couldn't help it—he loved women; the sexier, the better. He continued to stare at Nikki, captivated by what could be seen beneath her dress. "Damn," he muttered. *Bet you know how to have some fun in bed.*

"I take it you like what you see," Nikki teased.

Victor nodded. *"Seguro." It's a shame I won't have time to indulge.*

Nikki batted her eyes at him and flashed him a sultry smile.

He popped the trunk of the Roadster and motioned with his Beretta for Spence to approach him. "Take a look-see."

Spence lifted the trunk and glanced inside: two open duffel bags filled with money.

"Check the cash," Victor said.

Spence reached inside one of the bags and pulled out a stack of banded bills: all twenties. Separating a single note from the stack, he ran a handheld ultraviolet light over it to detect counterfeits. It looked good.

He reached into the other bag, sunk his hand in even deeper, and came up with another banded stack of notes separated by denomination. He performed the same spot check.

"See? No party packs, Mr. Taylor."

Spence zipped up the bags. "Everything seems to be in order." *"Bueno."*

Spence lifted the two duffel bags out of the trunk and walked over toward Nikki and Cordoza.

"Two days," Victor reminded them, holding up two fingers. "That's when Francisco expects to have his money."

"Two days," Cordoza repeated.

Seconds later, a dark-colored van sped into the parking lot and screeched to a halt. The side door slid open. Two men in black windbreakers jumped out. "Freeze! DEA!" they yelled, weapons drawn. "Get down now!"

Nikki and Cordoza froze.

"Setup!" Victor shouted. "You fucking bastards set me up!"

Spence dropped the duffel bags and reached for his semi-automatic. Several shots rang out, hitting him in the chest. He collapsed.

Nikki screamed.

Victor returned fire.

The DEA agents split up. One engaged him, while the other grabbed the money. Victor ducked behind his Roadster and squeezed off several more rounds. A return volley of gunfire ripped through the body of his Mercedes. He yanked open the door, fired off two more shots, and dove inside.

The second agent rejoined the fight, shooting in Victor's direction. Victor hunched down behind the wheel. Rounds whizzed past his head and struck the windshield. Spider-web cracks appeared, stretching across the length of the glass. Victor peeped over the dashboard. He spotted Nikki and Cordoza hopping back into their SUV. He extended his firearm out the window and blindly shot in their direction until he was out of ammo. As the DEA continued to close in, he stomped down on the accelerator and sped out of the kill zone into the busy streets.

CHAPTER FIFTEEN

The Denali sped through the Compound's gate and came to a screeching halt in front of the portico. Cordoza jumped out of the SUV, opened the rear door, and dragged Nikki out by the hair. She screamed as he marched her into the lobby.

"You're hurting me," she squealed.

Cordoza shoved her up against the wall, hard. A stone-cold expression etched itself across his face. "Did you blow the deal?" he asked, pointing Spence's gun at her.

"Spence is on the pavement, bleeding out, and you're wondering if I blew the deal. Did *you* blow the deal?"

Cordoza laughed. "I've spent the last six months putting us in a position to get a deal, so I don't think I'm a leading contender here."

Nikki shook her head in disbelief. "Listen to yourself. Do you hear what you're saying?"

Cordoza pressed the barrel of Spence's gun against Nikki's head. "I'm not going to ask you again. Did you sell us out?"

Nikki felt the pressure of the cold steel against her temple but didn't react. Their eyes locked. "Gem," she said softly, "I didn't do it, I swear."

He moved his face to within inches of hers. "I don't believe you." His breath was hot and smelled of cigars.

Nikki let out a deep breath. "Damn it, you wouldn't have a deal if I hadn't swayed Vicente to do business with us."

"True, but only four people on our crew knew about the meet: Spence, Willard, you, and me. Spence is gone, and Willard's whereabouts can be accounted for, so that leaves just you."

"You know me, Gem. You can trust me." Nikki hoped she sounded convincing.

"You just did three and a half years in prison. You come; you go. How do I know you're not whispering sweet songs about my operation into your parole officer's ear?"

Nikki laughed at the implication. "You invite me back, tell me how desperately you need my help, and now I'm your Judas?"

Cordoza nodded. "It adds up for me."

"I get it—you're spooked. I'm spooked too, so I'll forgive you for not thinking straight, but you're overlooking something."

Cordoza loosened his hold a little but still kept her pinned against the wall. "And what's that?"

"Your math."

Cordoza gave her a disgruntled look.

"Spence, Willard, and I weren't the only ones who knew that deal was going down."

"What do you mean?"

Nikki took a deep breath and gained her composure. "Lacey—she was in the room too. You want to talk about somebody coming and going...where is she right now?"

"Yoga class," he snapped.

"You sure about that?"

Cordoza hesitated. "Okay, maybe at the herbalist. I get that new age bullshit mixed up all the time."

Cordoza released his hold on her, took a step back, and lowered the weapon.

"Thank you," she said, grateful to be free. He didn't reply.

"Now, if you'll excuse me, I'll be up in my room, scanning the local channels for news coverage about the raid."

Cordoza shook his head. "Let me know the minute you find something."

Nikki bolted for the elevators. Once she was back in her room, she turned on the TV but kept the volume on mute while she dialed the lifeline from her cell phone.

"Touch of Style Salon," a rosy voice announced. "How can I help you?"

Nikki rushed through the agent verification process in a whisper and waited for confirmation.

"Cousin Nikki, how are you?"

"Not too good. Could be better."

"I'm sorry to hear that. What's up?"

Shaken up, Nikki took a deep breath. "Janice..."

"Yes, honey."

Nikki paused. With Cordoza's suspicion aroused, she considered the possibility that he was eavesdropping on her just beyond the door.

"Cousin Nikki," Janice called out.

"I'm here."

"Go ahead, girl."

"I need to cancel breakfast," Nikki stated, using the code phrase to request an emergency meeting.

"No problem. I'll get back to you as soon as I figure out when we can hook up again."

"Thanks." Nikki hung up.

Several hours later, following directions Janice had given her, Nikki found herself in front of an out-of-the-way seamstress shop. She walked inside. A frumpy, gray-haired woman, wearing a smock with a tape measure draped around her neck, greeted her and escorted her to the back room. Inside, Harlan stood holding a plush roll of fabric several feet away from Special Agent Bolston while she pretended to stitch it.

"We got raided," Nikki announced.

Harlan set the textile roll down and turned toward her. "I know…I was there."

"I specifically requested a surveillance team to observe the exchange from the top of the adjacent parking deck, nothing more."

Kameko looked up from behind the industrial sewing machine.

Nikki waved. "So why'd you raid us, Harlan?"

His face drew a blank. "Raid you? I didn't authorize that bust. We were busy taking photos and gathering intelligence like we were supposed to."

"Cordoza's spooked," Nikki said. "Thinks I sold him out. Damn near tried to kill me."

Harlan's eyes widened. "Not good."

"Well, if you didn't raid us, who did?"

"That's something I need to look into and get back to you on."

"Start with the DEA and go from there," Nikki said. "What about Spence Taylor?"

Harlan took a deep breath then looked directly at her. "Dead."

Nikki gasped.

Harlan hesitated for a moment. "By the time we got down there…he was gone."

Nikki's stomach churned. She placed her hand over her mouth then shook her head. Overwhelmed by a hollow emptiness inside, she allowed so many pleasant memories of him to slip into her mind and fill the void: training Spence in the craft of ATM skimming, playing late-night games of chess to decompress after long hours of planning financially rewarding crimes, and shopping together for clothes at outlet stores uptown. Soon those thoughts dissipated, replaced by a bitter one: Spence shoving her to the ground to gain a sizable lead and avoid arrest by pursuing cops. The image of him offering her up as a sacrificial lamb still burned. Tears ran down Nikki's cheeks. She squeezed her eyes shut. "You're forgiven," she whispered. "I release you from that wrong."

Concerned, Harlan moved closer to her and touched her forearm lightly. "I'm sorry for your loss."

She looked away.

"Nicole, if there's anything I can—"

"Get to the bottom of this," she replied, wiping the tears from her face.

"Will do."

She reached into her purse and removed a bundled stack of cash.

Harlan's eyebrows rose. "What do we have here?"

"Five grand."

"For?"

Nikki handed the money to him. "Evidence."

Harlan nodded slowly. "I see."

"And don't think I wasn't tempted either," Nikki added. "Five grand could easily pay for a month's worth of Marty's care."

Harlan motioned for Kameko to come over. She emerged from behind the sewing machine and approached him. He handed the cash to her. "Log it."

Kameko flipped through the bills to get a count.

"Is that all, Nicole?" Harlan asked.

"No, a fifteen-hundred-dollar check for IT consulting, courtesy of the Cordoza crew."

Harlan held out his hand. Nikki dug into her purse again and pulled out a business envelope. She stared at it for a moment, hesitating to hand it over. *Take it before I spend it*, she thought.

Harlan motioned for the check. Nikki quickly gave it to him.

He opened the envelope and glanced over the bank draft. "Seems legit," he said, holding it out for Kameko to exam.

"It's real," she confirmed.

Harlan did a double take. "That was quick, Bolston."

"The numbers in the upper-right-hand corner match the last few digits on the MICR line. A consistent font runs throughout the check, and there's a perforated edge on the back as well as a bright bank logo that's difficult to duplicate."

"All righty then."

"Secret Service, Harlan," Kameko teased. "It's part of what we do: identify, track, and put a stop to counterfeiting."

A smug expression slid over Harlan's face. He pulled the check back, took out his cell phone, and snapped a picture of the draft. Then he placed the check back in the envelope. "Here," he said, handing it to Nikki.

She took it and placed it in her purse.

Harlan wiggled the side of his glasses. "Cash it."

Nikki's eyebrows shot up. "Okay."

"Cordoza's already suspicious of you. He's gonna be looking for this check to clear, so let's not play into his paranoia by not cashing it."

"Will do."

Kameko reached into her tweed jacket and removed a USB flash drive from her pocket. "My top guys took a look at this," she told Nikki. "It took a lot of brainstorming, but they managed to solve your problem by leveraging the key-holder index system."

Nikki cast a blank look Kameko's way. "Key-holder index system?"

"Yes, you're familiar with the Title Three restrictions of the Patriot Act, right?"

Nikki nodded. "Ten-thousand-dollar cap on all financial transactions. Anything above that must be reported to the government."

"Well, that's not entirely true."

Nikki squinched her face up in surprise.

"Within the US financial system, there are a group of individuals, twenty-six in all, who have the government's 'blessing' to move large amounts of currency unencumbered. These people are known as key holders."

"Doesn't that defeat the purpose of having a Title Three section of the Patriot Act?" Harlan asked.

"Not necessarily," Kameko said. "All the key holders are highly vetted. Some of them even hold positions in the upper echelons of government."

"You mean the deep, dark corners nobody dares to go looking in."

Kameko frowned at Harlan for making the insinuation. "Yes."

"Pretty much explains the infinite number of CIA slush funds and the nine lives they seem to have."

Nikki interrupted their banter. "How does this key-holder index system get my money-laundering program to work?"

"We took reserve digital authorization codes from the index, placed them in a self-modulating matrix, then embedded it within a reverse shell," Kameko explained. "Once banking security application software has been breached, the DNS settings will be altered and set to a primary server the Secret Service controls. From there, we can monitor the program as it taps into the ACH Network, providing recognized digital override codes. If we encounter any hiccups, we can course-correct with direct commands from the home office. It's smooth sailing from there."

Nikki smiled. "Kinda of like an E-Z pass for road tolls."

"Hardly," Kameko scoffed. "More like carte blanche at Saks Fifth Avenue. You'll be able to manipulate currency amounts, denominations, number of accounts, and the location of funds."

"Amazing."

Kameko handed Nikki the flash drive. "And now I present to you the Spectral Drive," she said, with a flourish of her hand.

A curious look spread across Nikki's face. "As in a ghost or phantom?"

"Yep, this thing is so smooth it's virtually undetectable. My guys did an excellent job. The best part is that once the digital override codes have been activated, we'll be able to track the money no matter where it ends up. We've basically created a digital beacon that attaches itself to the funds being laundered."

"Brilliant. Sounds like we have a winner here."

"I'd like to think so," Kameko said, grinning. "This will allow us to see the overall big picture, who's doing business with who, and alert us to new players in the game. The possibilities are endless."

"So basically we'll be fishing digitally," Harlan commented.

Kameko nodded.

"Using Cordoza as a proxy," Nikki said. "He brings in Quinn; Quinn leads us to Vicente, and so forth and so on."

"Exactly. That's why it's important for us to find out why this deal went sour and salvage it. If we can fulfill the brokering contract by completing the transaction, law-enforcement agencies everywhere could reap the benefits for years to come from our work here today."

The frumpy, gray-haired woman who had escorted Nikki to the back room returned. She was accompanied by a slender Latina woman dressed in corporate gray and clutching a leather business portfolio.

All eyes shifted to her. She stepped forward and extended her hand toward Nikki. "Nicole Frank? Melinda Procter, legal clerk for the office of US Attorney GW Strickland."

"Pleased to meet you," Nikki said, shaking her hand. *I hope this is about Marty*, she thought.

"Likewise."

"What can I do for you?"

Melinda opened up the zippered folder and removed a digital audio recorder. "I'm here to take your sworn statement on the alleged abuses currently under investigation at the Madelyn P. Shaw Women's Correctional Facility."

"Sure," Nikki said, trying to mask her disappointment.

"For your protection, Ms. Frank, we'll list you as a reliable confidential informant on all documentation presented to the grand jury for review."

Nikki nodded that she understood.

"Raise your right hand," Melinda said, pressing "record" on the voice recorder. "And repeat after me."

Nikki raised her hand.

"I, Nicole Marie Frank..."

"I, Nicole Marie Frank..."

"Do solemnly swear..."

"Do solemnly—"

Nikki's phone rang. "Sorry. I have to take this," she said, assuming it was Cordoza. "Give me a second."

Melinda shut off the recorder. Nikki opened her purse and fished out her phone. "Hello?"

"Nikki?"

"Yes," she replied tucking her hair behind her ear.

"Emma from Paris Oaks."

"Hey, I—"

"It's about Marty."

Nikki's face crumpled up. "What is it?"

"He's missing."

CHAPTER SIXTEEN

Victor stepped off the elevator, stopped in front of his suite, and called Quinn. The phone rang several times before he answered it.

"Patrone here," Victor said.

"What is it?"

"We've been hit."

"Shit," Quinn hollered. "When?"

"About thirty minutes ago."

"By who?"

"DEA."

"And the money?"

"Gone."

Quinn sighed. "All of it?"

"Yes."

"You've got to be fucking kidding, Patrone."

Victor didn't respond.

"Where are you now?"

"En route to the yacht," he lied.

"Good. I'll see you when you get here."

Victor hung up and swiped his key card through the door reader. A green light appeared, disengaging the lock. He turned the handle and entered the suite. Inside, Onyx, Topaz, and Jasper sat in a semicircle around two open duffel bags.

Topaz reached down into one, grabbed a few bundles of cash, and held them up for Victor to see. "We hit the mother lode, *esé*."

Victor smiled. "We certainly did."

"Now these are the muthafucking jobs you need to be contracting us fo'," Onyx added. "Not that penny-pinching shit for Q."

Victor turned to Jasper. "Did you get rid of the van?"

"Firebombed it in some back alley."

The cartel lieutenant raised an eyebrow, prompting Jasper to elaborate.

"Molotov cocktails. When they do find it, there won't be much left."

"And the DEA jackets?"

"Tossed."

"What about the champagne?"

Jasper grinned. "On ice in the guest bathroom."

Victor gave the trio an approving nod. "Outstanding."

"Just like you muthafucking requested," Onyx chimed in.

"Well, if y'all will excuse me, I'll fetch the bubbly." Victor headed down the hallway and stepped into the bathroom.

The tub was filled with ice. Several bottles of Möet & Chandon Imperial were dispersed throughout the basin. Victor shut the door, pulled out his phone, and hit speed dial. Lacey picked up.

"I'm…" Victor hesitated for a second. "I'm sorry for hurting you."

Lacey didn't respond.

"That wasn't me. Honest, sweetheart. It's just…sometimes you can be—"

"What?" Lacey demanded. "I can be what?"

Victor sighed. "Cold."

"That doesn't give you the right—"

"I know, I know."

Lacey let out a heavy sigh. "What you did disgusts me."

"Do you remember the place we first met?" Victor asked.

"Yeah."

"We need to meet there now."

"What for? What's the point?"

"So I can make it up to you…in a big way. I promise."

There was a long pause.

"Sweetheart?"

"I'm here."

"Well?"

"Fine," Lacey said. "I'll meet with you."

Victor hung up, then placed the phone on the vanity counter top. He withdrew his Beretta from the holster underneath his arm and reloaded the weapon. When he finished, he affixed a sound suppressor to the barrel, walked back into the living room, and pointed the semiautomatic at the group. A wide-eyed look of surprise leapt from one man's face to another.

"*Esé*," Topaz pleaded.

"Gentlemen, thank you for your service," Victor said, ignoring the appeal, "but this is where we part ways."

"Muthafucker!" Onyx yelled.

Victor flashed a sly grin then opened fire. "Good help is so hard to find."

CHAPTER SEVENTEEN

The following morning, there was still no media coverage about the DEA bust. Nikki lied to Cordoza, telling him that her parole officer had heard about a large monetary seizure by the Feds and wanted her to report in for questioning, since the crime fit her known pattern of criminal behavior. Instead she had used the opportunity to meet with Harlan and Kameko at the seamstress shop. In the back of her mind, she wondered what was going on with Marty. The phone call from Emma had left her feeling frantic. Nikki was in a no-win situation. She had to stay close to Cordoza to maintain the illusion of being a loyal associate or risk being found out. This meant that Marty and whatever was going on at Paris Oaks had to be placed on hold.

While she was out, Cordoza had confined himself to his office and pored over his financials to determine if he had the cash flow to cover Vicente's loss.

"I simply don't have it," he confessed to Nikki, once she had returned to the Compound. "What did you turn up on your end?"

She looked around the office. It had changed. Gone were the battered desk, folding chairs, and home-improvement-store book shelves from five years ago. In its place were a mahogany L-shaped desk with a matching bookcase, two wing-back guest chairs, and a set of hand-carved wooden cabinets. The dull beige wall color had been replaced with a warm, inviting golden hue, accentuated with contrasting carpet.

Nikki pulled back one of the guest chairs and took a seat. "Absolutely nothing. Complete waste of time. You'd think a bust like that would be the talk of the town. Here it is, a day after the fact, and no chatter, no nothing. My PO was more concerned about the color of my urine sample than the possibility that I could've been a party to a recent crime."

Cordoza's cell phone rang. He shook his head. "Unknown Caller" flashed across the screen. He frowned. "Hello," he answered.

"We need to talk," a stern voice said.

"Who's this?"

"Quinn."

Cordoza silently cursed upon hearing the name of the city's premier drug lord. "Yes, sir. What can I do for you?"

"At the moment, nothing, but when I arrive—"

"Arrive?"

"That's right. Your groundskeeper just let me through the gate. I'll be there shortly."

Quinn hung up.

Cordoza stood up from behind his desk and rushed over to the cabinet to his left.

"Gem," Nikki called out, concerned.

He ignored her, opened several drawers, and rifled through them.

"What is it?" Nikki pressed.

"Where is it?" Cordoza mumbled. "Where the hell is it?"

Nikki stood. "Where's what? You're freaking me out."

Cordoza reached deep into the last compartment and pulled out a 1911 Colt .45. "Aha!"

Nikki's eyes narrowed. "Gem, what's going on?"

"Quinn," he replied, removing the pistol's magazine. "He's here."

"Now?"

Cordoza fumbled around with some loose rounds in the drawer and loaded the weapon. "Yeah."

Nikki stared at him, stunned. "Hasn't there been enough bloodshed already?"

Cordoza shrugged. "Maybe, but I'm not going down easily."

Nikki approached Cordoza and placed her hand over the semiautomatic to prevent him from continuing to load it. "Let's hear what Quinn has to say before we make things worse."

Cordoza chuckled. "Hear what he's got to say?" he repeated. "We lost two and a half million dollars of his boss's money. What's there to say?"

Nikki snatched her hand back toward her side.

A loud cough interrupted the two. Willard stood in the doorway, accompanied by two men. "Mr. Quinn and his associate, Tony Chen, sir."

Cordoza dropped the semiautomatic into the drawer. "Thank you, Willard."

The visitors stepped inside his office and looked around. They resembled Laurel and Hardy: the associate, long, lithe, and lean, while the kingpin was heavyset.

"We have a problem," Quinn announced. "A huge one."

Nikki glanced at Cordoza. He looked alarmed, though he tried to play it cool. *Please don't wig out now, Gem.*

"I'm out two and a half million dollars."

"Yes, sir," Cordoza murmured. "I realize that."

"And on top of that," Quinn added, "you can't fulfill Vicente's contract."

Cordoza shook his head then hung it low. "We got busted."

"That's what my man, Patrone, tells me." Quinn adjusted his

silk tie then moved toward one of the empty chairs. "Isn't it amazing how everything but the money managed to walk away?"

"Not everyone walked away," Nikki corrected. "We lost a close colleague."

Quinn massaged the back of the chair he was standing behind. "My condolences, but that doesn't change the fact that the first thing that should have sprouted legs and made it to safety was the two and a half million."

Quinn's bodyguard, Tony, snickered.

Nikki flashed him a dirty look. *Douche.*

"Now," the narcotics underboss continued, "I'm only gonna ask this once."

Tony reached inside his Mandarin jacket, pulled out a Sig Sauer P239, and pointed it at Nikki and Cordoza.

"Where's the money?" Quinn said.

A stunned look registered on Cordoza's face. "We don't have it. Like I said, we were about to do the exchange when the Feds raided us."

Quinn ran his thumb and index finger over his goatee. "Then what?"

"It was a madhouse," Nikki answered. "Gunfire from every direction. Spence gets shot; the DEA snatches up the loot; and your boy Patrone hightails it out of there."

Quinn motioned for Tony to lower his weapon. "I see." Nikki and Cordoza stared at each other, confused by the gesture. "Relax," Quinn reassured them. "I'm not going to kill you—at least not yet."

Tony snickered again.

"I just wanted to hear your side of the story."

Nikki crossed her arms. "Now that you have, what's next?"

Again, Quinn ran his fingers over his goatee. "We find Patrone, get his side of the story, then figure out who to kill."

Cordoza cringed. "Your guy's missing?"

"Yep, he was supposed to return back to the yacht yesterday after the exchange."

Tony tucked his P239 back inside the waistband underneath his jacket. "The boss here doesn't like to leave the yacht, so he's a tad bit pissed with this whole situation."

Nikki glanced at Cordoza again. He appeared less agitated now that the firearm had disappeared.

"I've had my suspicions about Patrone," Quinn admitted. "Ever since an independent team of accountants made me aware of the possibility that someone within my organization was skimming cash from our profits."

Nikki frowned. "I get it." Quinn raised an eyebrow. "You're still on the fence about us, right?"

"Precisely."

"Wondering if we had something to do with this?"

Quinn nodded.

"We didn't," Cordoza cut in.

The drug baron scrunched his face up into a knot.

Nikki quickly raised her hand up in front of Cordoza to signal him to back off. "Mr. Quinn, what can Mr. Cordoza and I do to alleviate your suspicions?"

A smile appeared across Quinn's face. He leaned in toward Tony and whispered something.

Nikki dropped her hand to her side and waited for a response.

"I propose," Quinn said, pointing to her, "that you and my man, Tony here, work together to find Patrone."

Nikki's eyes widened. "Me?"

"Yes, you."

She hesitated for a moment. *That's insane*, she thought.

"She's all yours," Cordoza offered.

Quinn's face burst into a sharp grin. "Excellent. Then we'll proceed together from here on out."

CHAPTER EIGHTEEN

Quinn insisted on speaking with Cordoza alone. Nikki excused herself and headed toward the lobby en route to her suite. The automated glass doors to the entrance hall opened, sending a blast of lukewarm air into the foyer. Lacey walked in clutching several shopping bags from Nordstrom, her eyes sparkling. Nikki noticed her new earrings and an expensive silk scarf wrapped around her head, tied in a rosette style.

"Well, well, well," Nikki said, smirking. "Look who's here! It's been ages."

Lacey's face turned sour. "You really shouldn't concern yourself with my comings and goings. It's unbecoming."

"Cute. We're in the middle of an unprecedented crisis, and you've got time to go shopping."

"Jealous?"

"Over what? A few shopping bags, some earrings, and an atrocious scarf?"

Lacey dropped a few of the bags and placed her hand on her hip. "This is a one-of-a-kind Roberto Cavalli floral print."

"Whatever."

"Have Spence and Willard grab the rest of my things out of the back of the Porsche and take them up to the penthouse."

Nikki didn't move.

Lacey motioned for her to shoo along.

Nikki stared at her for several more moments. Finally, her eyes lowered. "Spence is dead," she announced. The statement was flat—no emotion behind it.

Lacey looked stunned. "What?"

"Spence is dead." *What part don't you understand, you imbecile?*

"Come on."

Nikki didn't respond.

Lacey shook her head as tears formed in the corners of her eyes. "This can't be happening. I was just ribbing him about that damn computer program of his and whether or not it would work."

For a split second, Nikki felt a tad bit sorry for Lacey; nobody had thought to inform her of the loss. But then she recalled how Lacey consistently went out of her way to create a toxic environment, and the thought was forgotten.

Cordoza entered the lobby with Quinn and Tony. He spotted Lacey and walked toward her. The two locked eyes.

"Gemini, what's going on?" she asked.

Cordoza placed his arm around her, pulled her over to the side, and explained that they'd been raided by the Feds during the money drop. Nikki watched with interest as the couple's bizarre relationship dynamic unfolded before her eyes. She was convinced, now more than ever, that Cordoza was being manipulated.

Quinn picked up on Nikki's distraction and signaled Tony to approach her. He made a brisk move toward her. Startled, Nikki took a step back and crouched into a low defensive stance. "Whoa," she said, clenching her fists. "What do you think you're doing, rolling up on me like that?"

The tall Asian man with olive-green eyes lifted his hands high in the air. "My apologies...I didn't mean to spook you."

Nikki relaxed her hands and stood up straight. *I've sent women to the infirmary for less*, she thought grimly.

"It's time to get started," Tony said.

"Okay, Mr....umm?"

"Chen."

Nikki nodded. "Mr. Chen."

"Not Mr. Chen," Tony corrected. "Just Chen."

Nikki gave him a lackluster smile. *With those exotic good looks, you should be on a magazine cover.*

"My bad," Nikki apologized.

Tony extended his hand. "And you?"

Nikki clasped it and shook firmly. "Frank."

A puzzled look crossed Tony's face.

"Frank, Nikki Frank, but since we don't know each other like that, Frank will do," she insisted.

"Frank it is then."

Quinn approached the two, interrupting the conversation.

"Yes, boss?" Tony said.

"You two"—Quinn pointed at both of them—"start at Paris Oaks Assisted Living Facility and go from there."

Nikki's eyes grew wide. "An assisted living facility?"

Quinn snapped his head in her direction. "Is that going to be a problem?"

"Um," she mumbled. "No."

"'Cause if it's going to be a problem..."

Tony removed the P239 from his waistband.

Nikki stared at the semiautomatic. "It won't be a problem."

"Excellent," Quinn said, running his fingers over his goatee.

CHAPTER NINETEEN

Nikki parked the Buick in an open visitor's space and cut the ignition.

"What's so special about this place?" she asked Tony, feigning any knowledge of Paris Oaks. "Why does Quinn want us to start here?"

Tony tensed up at the questions. "An outside auditing firm made the boss aware of some irregularities on our books. He suspected Patrone of stealing and set him up with a test to either confirm his guilt or clear him."

"What kind of test?"

"A greenback end-around."

Nikki knew "greenback" was slang for "cash," and "end-around" pertained to a play in organized football. More specifically, it's a plan of action to advance the ball farther down the field by having the quarterback hand the ball off directly to the wide receiver. The receiver then proceeds to either run the ball, as directed, toward the line of scrimmage for more yards, or come up with something totally off the cuff to salvage a play that's crumbling fast.

Nikki concluded that Quinn was the quarterback and Patrone the wide receiver. "How much green?" she asked.

"Fifteen grand," Tony replied, pointing to the main building of the assisted living facility. "Right here, to this institution, as a charitable contribution."

Nikki shot Tony a quizzical look, her eyebrows raised and head tilted slightly. "Fifteen K?"

"That was the play Quinn called."

"Whew."

"Now we just need to find out what Patrone did with the ball."

Tony opened the door and stepped out of the car. "You really should consider getting rid of this clunker or at least paying to have it fixed up." Nikki simply nodded, trying to pull off a demure smile, although she didn't do "reserved" especially well. Tony headed toward the facility's entrance. Nikki followed, putting on a pair of sunglasses. Tony turned toward her. "Listen up, Frank," he said in a stern voice. "I do the talking here; you just hover in the background."

Nikki nodded then forced a smile. *Hover in the background?* That's all she'd thought about on the drive over: how best to go unnoticed in a familiar setting where she was known. She had weighed all the options, including telling Tony that her brother was a resident here, a consideration she dismissed quickly. *Cartels are notorious for extending violence to family members*, she thought. *If I'm ever outed…Marty didn't sign up for this—I did. I've already compromised his safety with Gem. I won't do it again.* Nikki decided, in this scenario, she would have to improvise and roll with the flow.

Inside the lobby, Bethany, the redheaded receptionist, was steadily typing at her curved mahogany workstation.

Tony approached the desk. Nikki cringed. This was the most dangerous part of undercover work, the crossroads—the point at which her personal life, professional life, and criminal life all merged. She could be exposed right here, which could cause things to unravel fast.

"Excuse me," Tony said, interrupting the receptionist.

Nikki's heart leaped.

Bethany glanced up at Tony, sighed, then went right back to typing. "Yes."

Nikki felt a slight sense of ease; Bethany's preoccupation with her work had prevented her from being immediately recognized.

Tony sighed. "I'm here to follow up on a charitable contribution," he said.

Nikki's anxiety ratcheted up a notch. Tony's request for information increased her odds of exposure. At any minute, Bethany would stop what she was doing and give him her undivided attention. At that moment, Nikki would be remembered and a comment or two about her brother and/or his situation would be voiced. She would then either have to feign ignorance or be up-front with all parties. Neither option was acceptable. Nikki had to prevent Tony from learning about Marty. Risk management demanded it. If anything ever happened to him, she'd never forgive herself.

Bethany didn't budge but continued to sit behind her workstation and type.

"Look, you redheaded bitch," Nikki said, raising her voice, "stop what you're doing right now and assist the gentleman addressing you."

Nikki hoped to shock the receptionist, the goal being to prevent the careless revelation of their past association. It was an old trick used by debt collectors: get consumers upset and use their emotional state against them to get them to pay up. In this case, Nikki was counting on the emotional impact of her colorful language and Bethany's "professionalism" to neutralize the imminent threat posed by idle chitchat.

A stunned look spread across Bethany's face. She glared at Nikki.

Nikki stared back. "We're waiting."

Bethany stood up. "My apologies, sir. What was your question again?"

"I'm here to follow up on a charitable contribution," Tony repeated.

He withdrew his cell phone from his jacket and scanned through a variety of photos until he found one of Patrone. "Have you seen this guy in the last forty-eight hours?" he asked, holding up the phone.

The receptionist hesitated for a moment. "I'm not at liberty to say."

Nikki cut her another scathing look.

"Yes," she said, quickly changing her mind. "He passed through here a day or two ago."

"The man you identified," Tony continued, "was tasked by my employer to make a generous donation to your institution on his behalf."

Bethany's face tightened.

"Bethany," Tony said, reading her name off the glass plate on her desk, "how much did my colleague contribute?"

Bethany just stood there, staring straight at him. Behind her was a corridor that branched off into several offices and ended with a midsize conference room. There, Nikki spotted Emma. The two made eye contact. Emma looked worried, possibly scared. Her hand covered her mouth, and she was shaking her head. Nikki assumed it had to do with Marty, but she couldn't tell at the moment.

"Bethany," Tony yelled.

The receptionist jumped.

"How," he said, deliberately slowly and drawn out, "much?"

"I'm not at—"

"Fine, you don't have to say a word. Just indicate the amount with your hands."

Bethany's eyes shifted back and forth while she contemplated her response. Finally, she lifted her hand and flashed Tony five fingers.

He turned to Nikki and whispered, "I need to touch base with Quinn and report my findings. Wait here."

She nodded and watched as he stepped out of the building.

Once the door shut, Nikki bolted past Bethany toward the conference room.

Emma stood inside, against the wall, her eyes shut as she massaged her temples. She jumped when the door burst open.

"It's just me," Nikki said, shutting the door behind her and removing her sunglasses.

Emma took a deep breath, and then the two hugged like long-lost sisters.

"What's the latest on Marty?" Nikki asked, breaking the embrace. "Did you find him?"

Emma bit her lower lip. "The staff and I have checked his room, his favorite spots, and his last-known whereabouts, but we've come up with nothing. Mrs. Ruiz has notified the police and is in direct contact with them now."

Nikki glanced up at the wall clock. She was pressed for time. Soon, Tony would be back in the building, and her absence would garner scrutiny. Nikki thanked Emma for the update and cracked open the door.

"Wait," Emma said.

Nikki paused, turning back toward her.

"I adore your brother, and I've become quite fond of you," Emma confessed. "I know this is none of my business, but I'll say it anyway."

A look of concern spread across Nikki's face. "What is it?"

"The guy you're here with…"

"Yeah?"

"He's bad news, real bad news."

"I know," Nikki replied. *But how do you? Former lover?*

Emma's eyebrows shot up. "Oh."

"Anything else?"

Emma shook her head. "Just be careful."

Nikki gave her a nod. "I will."

She smiled back. "Call me if you run into trouble."

CHAPTER TWENTY

Tony pointed to an empty parking lot where a wiry man in a navy-blue suit stood next to an idling police cruiser in the distance. Nikki slowed down, turned into the space, and came to a complete stop. "Who is this again and why are we meeting with him?"

Tony shook his head. "You sure ask a lot of questions."

"Wouldn't *you*? My associate is dead. My crew has been ripped off, and—"

"*We*," Tony corrected. "*We've* been ripped off."

Nikki blinked in surprise. "And to top it all off, I'm on parole. So yes, my risk meter is on sensory overload." Tony laughed. "Some answers would be nice, you know?"

Tony motioned for her to drive forward. She felt a tinge of apprehension in her gut but eased off the brake and steered the Buick into the slot next to the police cruiser. *Now what?*

"Don't look so worried," Tony said, observing her body language. "He's on the payroll."

Nikki's mouth fell open.

Tony chuckled. "Things run a helluva lot smoother when you've got an inside man."

The pair got out of the Regal and approached the cruiser. Nikki scanned the area for suspicious activity, while Tony headed for the officer. The cop recognized Tony instantly. "Who's the chick? And what's up with the fucked-up ride?"

"For now, she's my partner," Tony answered. "At least until the boss says otherwise. I can't speak to the car."

The officer gave Nikki a good up-and-down glance, followed by a favorable nod.

"I'm glad I meet with your approval," Nikki quipped. *Creep.*

The officer frowned at the remark.

"She can be a handful at times," Tony added. "Just ignore it."

Nikki rolled her eyes.

Tony chuckled. "So what you got for me, Bosky?"

The lieutenant scratched his head. "Not much. Quinn called, wanted me to check into whether the Feds had any live operations going on in the area and told me to assist you as much as possible."

"And?"

Bosky shrugged. "Nothing so far. What's exactly going on here?"

Tony tensed up. "Patrone and two and a half million dollars."

Bosky shook his head and sighed.

"Both are missing."

"Can't say I'm surprised."

Tony raised an eyebrow.

"Bastard was blackmailing me for twenty percent of my kick-back with compromising photos of my daughter."

That seemed to get Tony's attention. "Oh, really?"

"Yeah."

"Now there's a class act," Nikki said with a hint of sarcasm.

Tony motioned for Bosky to continue.

"Apparently my daughter got caught up with some unsavory characters on campus who were operating an amateur—"

The sound of two emergency alert tones from the squad car interrupted Bosky.

"Vehicle fire with explosions," the dispatcher announced. "Warwick and Thirty-Fifth Street. Dark-blue van, government tag G772361."

The radio crackled with some brief static.

"Two eighteen en route," a unit replied instantly.

"Two twenty-nine trailing," broadcast another.

The radio crackled once again.

"Forty-two Direct," the dispatcher called out. "Come in. Over."

Bosky sighed. "Hold on. I need to take this."

Tony nodded.

The lieutenant reached inside the cruiser and grabbed the handheld mike. "Forty-two Direct, copy. Units two eighteen and two twenty-nine rolling."

"Affirmative. Fire is already on the scene."

"Ten-four."

Nikki's cell phone rang. "Frank," she answered.

"Touch of Style Salon. Please stand by for an account representative."

Nikki recognized Janice's voice and waited for Harlan to be patched through.

"Nicole," he said.

"Yes?"

"No luck on any large monetary seizures in the area, federal or local."

Nikki hung her head. "I see."

"Whatever's going on, it's playing down at your level."

"I understand."

"Be careful," Harlan warned.

Nikki hung up and lifted her head.

Tony locked eyes with her. "Who was that?"

A sour look spread across Nikki's face. "My hair stylist. Why?"

"You seem distracted."

"Maybe."

"Look, I need you one hundred percent focused on what we're doing," he said, gesturing back and forth between Nikki and himself. "Got it?"

"You mean, like picking up from the radio traffic that a government van was recently torched and concluding that it could quite possibly have something to do with our situation."

Tony's eyes widened. "Exactly."

"Lesson learned. Now let's get to Warwick and Thirty-Fifth ASAP."

CHAPTER TWENTY-ONE

The van was on its side, in the middle of a back alley, five blocks from the central business district. Smoke and flames burst out of it, billowing up into the sky. One of the first responders pulled a fire extinguisher from his cruiser and attempted to gain control of the blaze. When the extinguisher ran dry, the vehicle fire reignited. Several ominous pops went off in quick succession, followed by a shower of sparks.

The wail of sirens intensified. Additional responders arrived. Nikki and Tony stood about a hundred feet away, watching. The firefighters went to work dousing the flames with sprayable foam.

The stench of burning rubber and gasoline saturated the air. Nikki gagged. Tony grabbed her by the arm and pulled her past the police barricade. An officer cut them off. Tony stopped.

"Exactly where are you two going?" Officer Hardy asked.

Nikki pointed straight ahead. "Over there."

"Not today, you aren't. For your safety, you'll have to remain behind the barricade."

Tony let out an audible sigh.

Officer Hardy motioned toward his holster. "Problem?"

The two locked eyes for a moment.

"Not at all," Tony said, breaking eye contact. "Not at all."

"I didn't think so."

Nikki grabbed Tony and quickly ushered him back to the car.

"Fucking cops," he complained. "I hate 'em."

Nikki empathized with a nod. *What a cheap power play,* she thought, *threatening the use of deadly force to gain compliance.*

"Take a deep breath," she told Tony. "Relax."

Tony inhaled than exhaled.

Nikki raised an eyebrow. "Better?"

"For now."

"Cool." She pointed to the smoldering vehicle. "Chen, I'm almost certain this was the van that busted us. Look at the agency lettering on the side."

Tony glanced at the logo. It read "DEA" in bright-yellow letters.

"Okay," he said. "That's a start, but where do we go from here?"

Nikki shrugged.

"My thoughts exactly," said Tony.

Several hundred feet away, a homeless man was pushing a shopping cart down the street.

Nikki spotted him instantly. "Over there," she said, pointing in the opposite direction of the wreckage. "The bum with the buggy."

Tony nodded and smiled. "Wearing the DEA jacket?"

"Yeah, that's our lead."

"Good eye, Frank. Let's get over there before the cops notice him."

The two rushed over to the man. He wore desert camouflage pants and loud purple tennis shoes and reeked of alcohol and body odor. Nikki held her breath, which did little more than make her blue in the face.

"Hey, where'd you get that jacket?" Tony asked.

The haggard man glanced down at the windbreaker he was wearing, looked up, and stared past him in a daze. "Yo, man, you got some spare change so I can get somethin' to eat?"

Tony shook his head.

"Come on, Miyagi. I know you got somethin'."

Tony sneered at the epithet. "Hospitality is contingent on information," he replied.

The vagrant scratched his head. "Huh?"

"You want money," Nikki clarified, cutting in, "answer the question."

The man ran a hand across his grimy beard. "Oh…okay."

"Where'd you get the jacket?" Tony repeated.

"Dumpster."

"Which dumpster?"

"By them hotels," the man said, pointing left.

Nikki turned and looked in that direction. She spotted two towering pole signs in the distance, on opposite sides of the road. One read, grand hyatt hotel; the other, chateau regency.

"Pay him," Nikki said.

Tony reached inside his jacket, took out his billfold, and removed a crisp twenty-dollar bill. He smirked and held it up high. The homeless man smiled, revealing several missing teeth and a few remaining brown ones. Tony shook his head and dropped the note on the ground. The man scrambled for the money as Tony stepped aside and laughed.

Nikki shot him a scornful look. "Really, Chen? Did you have to do that?"

Tony looked at her in disbelief. "What? You thought I was gonna hand it to him?"

Nikki shook her head.

"Next time you pay, Ms. Touchy-Feely."

Nikki clenched her jaw. "You know, you're a real piece of work."

Tony cracked a smile. "Yeah, my mother seems to think so too."

CHAPTER TWENTY-TWO

Nikki and Tony walked a quarter mile, located several dumpsters, and combed through each of them. Nothing. Filthy and exhausted, they sat down on the curb in front of the last remaining one. Nikki's body ached. She glanced down at herself for the first time and realized that the cranberry scoopneck tee and blue jeans she was wearing were ruined.

"Flip you for it," Tony said, removing a double-tailed quarter from his pocket. Before Nikki could protest, he threw the coin up in the air and caught it. "Call it?"

"Heads," Nikki replied.

Tony slid his covering hand back; it was tails. "Looks like the honor is all yours, Frank."

Nikki stood up. "Freaking splendid."

Tony chuckled.

"This isn't funny," she said, walking over toward the dumpster.

Tony leaned back on a patch of grass and placed his hands behind his head. "No, sweetheart, but it is fair."

Nikki slowly slid the hatch open. The ripe stench of days' old trash shoved its way into her nostrils.

"Woo-hoo!" Tony cheered. "Smells like a doozy."

Nikki shook her head. The nauseating odor reminded her of the bum they'd talked to earlier. She gagged, feeling the contents of her stomach shift. *I'm a go-getter*, she thought. *Rotting refuse is my perfume.*

"Houston, do we have a problem?" Tony taunted.

Nikki smacked the side of the dumpster several times to scare off any vermin that might be inside. She took a deep breath, cinched her lips tightly, and climbed inside the bin. The smell intensified. She gagged once more, barely suppressing the urge to vomit. *Think fresh-baked cookies*, Nikki told herself. *Fresh-baked cookies, just out of the oven.*

The bottom of the dumpster was covered in slime and food scraps. Several shiny, black, knotted garbage bags were piled in heaps against the far wall. Next to them was a well-worn tire, three bags of wilting arugula, and a Pampers box filled with used diapers.

"Find anything?" Tony called out.

"Nothing yet," she shouted back.

She panned to her right, scrutinizing every silhouette. Immediately her eyes were drawn to several cases of expired Tropicana orange juice stacked in the corner. There, lying across the top box, were two jackets.

"Hot damn," Nikki yelled, picking them up.

Tony sprang to his feet and rushed over. "Whaddya got?"

"The jackpot." She tossed him the jackets then climbed out of the dumpster.

Together they spread the nylon windbreakers out on the ground. "DEA" was silkscreened in yellow block letters across the backs of the jackets.

Tony quickly rummaged through the pockets. "Bingo!" He held up a royal-blue key card with gold writing on it. "Says 'Chateau Regency.'"

Nikki grinned.

Tony handed her the card.

She examined it. "Guess this is our next stop." Nikki passed the card back to him then took a whiff of her shirt. She quickly pulled away, scrunching up her nose. "Showers first."

"Sure thing."

The two headed back to the car then stopped at Target to purchase clothing before freshening up at a twenty-four-hour gym.

Once they were inside the lobby of the Chateau Regency, Nikki and Tony exchanged a few words before she casually strolled up to the front desk with the key card in hand. Tony waited on a sofa near the entrance.

The clerk smiled. "Welcome to the Chateau Regency. How can I help you?"

Nikki glanced at the clerk's name tag. "Yes, Julian," she said, responding warmly. "I've forgotten my room number. I was wondering if you could look it up for me?"

"Sure, no problem. Please let me see your card."

Nikki handed Julian the card. He took it and slid it through the key reader linked to his desktop. "May I see a photo ID, please?"

Nikki dipped her chin to her chest. "Look, can I be candid here?"

"Go ahead," Julian said, glancing up from the screen to make eye contact.

"I'm here to see Victor Patrone."

Julian's eyebrows shot up. "Are you now? You a working girl?"

Nikki scowled. "No."

Julian pointed in Tony's direction. "I suppose that's your pimp lingering over there in the background."

Nikki glanced over her shoulder in time to catch Tony in midwave. "Absolutely not. He's an associate."

"Associate? Is that what they're calling it these days?"

"Look, I don't know what you think is going on here, but—"

"Mr. Patrone assured me that this activity would no longer continue on our premises."

"I'm not a call girl," Nikki insisted.

Julian picked up the desk phone.

Nikki's eyes grew wide. "What are you doing?"

"Calling someone to remove the trash, honey. This is a respectable establishment."

A scream interrupted the conversation. Julian dropped the phone. A housekeeping attendant, bursting from the emergency-exit stairwell, was running toward him.

"Jules, call 911," she said, out of breath.

He froze. "What?"

Nikki stepped aside, yielding her space in front of the reception desk to the distressed woman.

"Dead bodies," the housekeeper continued. "Three of them, blood all over the place."

It took a moment for Julian to register what she had said. "Where?"

The woman took a few more raspy breaths. "Top floor, room 1007."

Julian punched the information into the computer. The registration data appeared moments later. "The room is booked to... Victor Patrone."

Nikki signaled Tony to head to the elevators.

Julian quickly picked the dangling phone receiver up from the floor and dialed 911. "Don't you leave," he warned Nikki. "I'm sure the authorities will have some questions for both of you."

Nikki took a step back from the counter. "I think I've overstayed my welcome," she said, holding her hands up in a conciliatory gesture. "So if you'll excuse me, I need to be going."

Julian made a beckoning motion with his finger. "Get the hell over here."

Nikki ignored him and bolted for the elevators. Tony held one of the ascending cars open for her. "Which floor?" he asked.

"Ten."

Tony punched the button, and the door shut.

Nikki closed her eyes, took in a slow breath, and exhaled. *Three bodies, Patrone's room—this keeps getting better and better.*

"We got maybe five to ten minutes, tops," Tony announced, "before law enforcement shuts this whole place down."

The elevator came to a gentle stop, and the door slid open. Tony scanned the hallway then glanced at Nikki. "Room?"

"1007."

The two raced to the suite. The television was blaring, and the door was wide open. Tony stepped inside the room first. Nikki followed. As someone who'd never even watched her own blood being drawn, chances were good, she thought, that she might vomit. Nikki clenched her teeth to stifle the impulse. Inside, three male bodies littered the living-room floor. A mural of blood was splattered across the walls and carpet.

Nikki shook her head as she looked around the crimson-saturated scene. "What the hell happened here?" she asked, raising her voice.

Tony shot her an uneasy look.

Nikki grabbed the remote control and adjusted the television volume. "What?"

He shook his head.

"What is it, Chen?"

He still didn't respond.

Nikki watched his facial expression closely, searching for further clues. "You know these men, don't you?" she guessed.

Tony nodded. "Gemstone crew."

Nikki waited for a further explanation. When he didn't provide it, she circled her hand in a "continue" gesture. "And they are..."

"Hired muscle from Chicago," Tony finally said. "Independent contractors our crew uses from time to time."

"Their connection to Patrone?"

"My guess is he either hired them to pull the DEA stunt or someone else did."

Nikki placed her hand on her forehead. "Leading us to one of two possibilities: either they turned on each other or Patrone took them out."

Tony glanced up at the wall clock. "We need to hurry up and toss this place before the five-oh arrives."

Nikki stepped over two of the bodies and moved past the flat-screen TV to the far side of the room. She searched through a cabinet but found nothing of importance.

Tony disappeared down the hall and came back with a towel. "Use this," he said, tossing it to her. "Wipe down the area after you search it."

Nikki held up the towel. "Are you serious, in this day of modern forensics?"

"Yes," Tony replied, irritated. "The idea here is to make the cops work to establish a connection, not hand over the winning lotto ticket by making things easy for them."

A sly smile slipped across Nikki's face. "I hear you," she said. Tony vanished back down the hall into the master bedroom, while Nikki wiped down the cabinet she'd just searched and continued the shakedown. After sweeping across a work desk and bulldozing through a pair of end-table drawers and a chest, she found herself standing back over the bodies, rummaging through the TV credenza.

A news alert flashed across the screen: "Thirty-four-year-old man with Down syndrome missing from Paris Oaks Assisted Living Facility." Nikki stopped and continued to read the news ticker to herself: "Mr. Frank is five foot seven, has black hair and brown eyes and a slim to medium build. He was last seen wearing a Carolina Panthers windbreaker and black jeans. Anyone with any information about his whereabouts is asked to contact the Parkbridge Police Department." The scrolling news alert remained for a few more seconds then disappeared.

Marty, where are you?

Nikki pushed the thought to the back of her mind and went back to searching the console drawers. Something grabbed her ankle. She jumped. It was a hand, covered in blood. The grip grew tighter. One of the bodies had sparked back to life. Nikki dropped to her knees next to the man. His grip loosened, and his hand soon fell away. She instinctively checked his pulse. It was faint.

"Chen," Nikki called out.

Tony raced around the corner. "What is it?"

"This guy's alive, barely."

Tony rushed to the man's side. "Jasper, who did this to you?"

Jasper's eyes fluttered open.

"Jasper," Tony said again, this time louder.

Jasper's mouth trembled in an attempt to form words.

Nikki leaned in closer. "Talk to me, Jasper," she urged.

He mumbled a faint syllable. She lowered her ear further.

"Pa...trone"

"Patrone," Nikki repeated.

"Uh-huh." Jasper confirmed with a slight nod.

Nikki looked up at Tony. A cell phone went off. They both jumped.

"What the...?" Nikki said, startled.

Tony clenched his jaw. "Cell phone, Frank."

The phone continued to ring.

"Where?"

Tony moved back around the corner down the hall. "Sounds like the guest bathroom." He stepped inside and took a look around. There, on the marble counter top, was a Samsung. It continued to ring. Tony snatched it up. "Hello."

"Patrone?" a familiar voice said.

"Nah, boss, Tony."

"What?"

Tony leaned against the counter. "Yeah, I just found Patrone's phone in the guest bathroom of his suite at the Chateau Regency. Looks like he left it here to prevent anyone from tracking him."

"Find him," Quinn ordered.

"I'm—"

The click of the dead line cut Tony off. He shook his head, placed the phone inside his brand-new jacket, and rejoined Nikki out in the living room.

CHAPTER TWENTY-THREE

J ust as Nikki and Tony ducked back into the hallway, two uniformed patrol officers approached from the far side. "Freeze," the lead one yelled. "Don't move an inch."

The pair stopped immediately.

"You two again," Officer Hardy said, surprised.

Tony grimaced and shook his head.

Sergeant Twine walked over toward him. "Hope you didn't tamper with any evidence—"

"Not at all," Nikki said, cutting in before Tony could answer.

A cynical smirk flashed across Twine's face. "You know that's a felony," he continued, directing his attention over toward Nikki. "Don't you, little lady?"

The sergeant's demeaning remark riled her. "I'm not your little lady," she replied. "Are we clear?"

He ignored her question and asked his own. "Listen, dear, what were you two characters doing near that crime scene?"

"We heard the commotion and decided to check it out."

"Did you know any of the victims?"

Nikki looked over at Tony. The two locked eyes.

"Well?" the sergeant pressed.

"Well, what?" Nikki asked.

"Do you recognize any of the victims?"

"No," she lied.

Sergeant Twine shook his head, clearly not believing her. "Mm-hmm."

Nikki sneered. "Not a soul, honest."

"I find that hard to believe, little lady."

"Look, all I know is you've got one helluva mess on your hands in there."

Sergeant Twine shot her a stern look. "You two stay here in the hallway until we hear from the lead investigator. I'm sure he's gonna have some questions for both of you."

A grim look crossed Tony's face. He cursed under his breath.

"Officer Hardy," Twine called out.

"Yes, Sergeant?"

"Keep an eye on them while I check out the room."

"Aye, Sergeant."

Sergeant Twine disappeared into the room. Everyone stared at one another once he left. "You'd better hope the tampering in that suite is minimal," Officer Hardy warned. "Or I'll run both of you in on a litany of—" The crackle of his handheld radio cut him off. Hardy tugged the radio free from his utility belt. "Hardy. Go ahead. Over."

"Detective Mallorca here. Escort those persons of interests down to the front desk."

"Roger, Detective. En route now."

Nikki and Tony exchanged alarmed looks.

"All right, you two, let's step it out," Hardy ordered.

The pair moved down the hallway toward the elevators. Officer Hardy followed.

"This could get nasty," Tony whispered.

"Then keep quiet," Nikki suggested, "and let me do all the talking."

"Agreed."

"I'll keep it civil and straight to the point, Chen."

Officer Hardy leaned forward and pressed the elevator call button. "You know, with a seasoned detective, all that preplanning alibis and strategizing bullshit rarely works."

The elevator chime sounded, and the door slid open. Nikki and Tony stepped inside; Officer Hardy followed. The ride down was silent and uncomfortable. When the elevator doors slid back open, Hardy herded them toward the front desk. A tall black man with Flex Wheeler–size shoulders bursting through his gray tweed jacket stood waiting for them.

Detective Mallorca stared at the couple without moving; then he nodded toward Hardy before focusing back on the pair. "Look," he began, "I don't know who you two are—don't really care—but Lieutenant Bosky insisted that I be more than forthcoming with you both about my findings here."

Tony let out a loud sigh of relief.

The detective raised an eyebrow and paused for a second. "With that said—"

"Thank you," Nikki said. "We appreciate your help, Detective."

Mallorca accessed his digital tablet. "Room was originally registered to an Armando Viera for about a month. Most recently it's been registered to a Victor Patrone." He looked back up at Nikki then over to the front-desk clerk. "Julian here says they're one and the same person." He added, "No credit card on file, cash payments only. In addition, a silver Mercedes Roadster, license plate HS6146, was listed as the occupant's primary vehicle."

Tony gave Nikki a nod, confirming that the information about Victor's car was accurate.

"We're running the plates now." Mallorca made several swipes across the face of his tablet. "Security-cam footage of the lobby and the tenth floor show a frequent female guest, about five eight or five nine, bleached-blond hair, and stacked. My guess, local prostitute. She's consistently been in the company of a man

I assume to be Mr. Patrone. The footage is a bit grainy. We'll work on having the images cleaned up so they can be disseminated to the press. We need to find whoever did this as soon as possible."

"Can we take a look at the surveillance video?" Tony asked.

Mallorca looked straight at the front-desk clerk. "Roll the footage for 'em, Julian."

"All of it, Detective?"

"Every last frame."

Nikki and Tony joined Julian behind the counter.

"Officer Hardy," Mallorca called out.

The patrolman perked up. "Yes, Detective?"

"I'm headed upstairs to join Sergeant Twine and take a look around the suite before forensics arrives."

"Yes, sir."

"Those security tapes remain here. Understand?"

Hardy nodded. "Aye, sir."

CHAPTER TWENTY-FOUR

After twenty-minutes of reviewing surveillance footage, Nikki and Tony made an abrupt exit from the lobby. They said nothing until they reached the parking garage.

"Did you see what I saw?" Tony asked.

Nikki hit the flip-key remote and unlocked the Buick. "Yeah, Lacey clocking more time at the Regency than an employee working double shifts."

Tony chuckled. "I wonder what the connection between those two is? On the surface, it seems to be just sexual."

Nikki's phone rang. She pulled it out of her back pocket and glanced down at the screen. It was the beauty salon again. "I need to take this call," she told Tony. He nodded and got inside the car. Nikki backed away from the parking space for some privacy. "Frank here," she answered.

"Touch of Style Salon," Janice rattled off without preamble. "Please stand by for an account representative."

Nikki waited for Harlan to be patched through. It felt like forever.

"Nicole," he finally said.

"Yes."

"You missed your report-in window."

Nikki gritted her teeth. "I know, but things have been a little—"

Harlan cut her off. "Sitrep?"

"Cordoza and Quinn are now working together," she began, switching to a professional tone. "There's a dirty cop on Quinn's payroll, a Lieutenant Bosky. Quinn's ordered him to help Chen and me find Patrone and the money. We followed up leads to the Chateau Regency, where we ran across a suite full of dead bodies. The room was registered to Patrone. The lieutenant pulled some strings and was able to help Chen and me gain access to hotel surveillance footage, which we just reviewed."

"And?"

"Patrone was definitely there, but so was Lacey, Cordoza's girlfriend."

The line went silent for a moment. Nikki heard Harlan breathing. Finally, he spoke. "So Lacey and Patrone are working together?"

"It sure looks that way," Nikki replied. "And my brother is missing."

"I know."

Although Nikki wasn't surprised, she was comforted by the revelation. It was Harlan's job to "know." He was the field supervisor; his primary duty was to anticipate and meet the needs of his agents in the trenches.

"Any word on him?"

"Ever since you expressed concern over the DEA raid," Harlan said, "we've been tapped into the local PD, but no...no leads on your brother yet."

Nikki's heart crumbled at the news.

"I'm sending a rescue coordinator to the precinct," Harlan said. "She specializes in searching for the mentally disabled."

"I appreciate that."

"And a K-9 team is inbound from upstate to help with the effort."

"Thank you."

"Don't worry. We'll find him. Keep your head in the game, kid."

"Will do," Nikki replied. "Keep me posted."

She hung up and returned to the car. Tony was seated on the passenger side, toying with Patrone's phone. "Finished?" he asked, looking up at her.

Nikki plunked down in the driver's seat. "Yeah, what's going on with you?"

"Not much. Just messing with Patrone's phone," Tony said, continuing to press buttons on the device. "Hoping to gather new intel."

"Find anything?"

Tony shook his head. "Nothing yet." A few moments later, he shouted, "Yes!"

Nikki whirled her head in his direction. "What?"

"I just opened the lock screen."

"Not bad."

"How 'bout 'outstanding'?" Tony corrected. "That was a four-digit pin, with ten thousand possible combinations."

Nikki grinned. "And just how did you pull that off?"

"Started with the most common pins like 1234, 4321, 0007, 0000, 1111, 2222—you get the idea—and then I progressed to more difficult sequences. Guess what Patrone's pin was?"

"What?"

Tony smiled wide. "2580."

Nikki's face went blank. *And?*

"Get it?"

She shook her head.

Tony handed her the phone. "Look at the dial pad and locate the four numbers."

Nikki did as was instructed. A moment later a sparkle came over her eyes, and she broke into a partial grin. "The sequence of numbers forms a line straight down the center of the phone."

"Bingo!"

Nikki handed the phone back to Tony then started up the car. "Where to, Chen?"

"Let's find Lacey."

Nikki backed out of the parking space and drove out of the garage. After turning left on Fox Canyon Road, past the Chateau Regency sign, she came to a complete stop at the intersection of Penrose and Fletcher. A text-message chime went off. It was the Samsung. Tony glanced down at the phone in his hand: incoming text, unidentified number. The message read: "You're late! Rivercrest Square, Promenade."

Tony turned to Nikki. "Change of plans. Rivercrest Square."

"I'm on it," she replied, changing directions.

Traffic heading toward the outdoor mall was busy. Cars and trucks jockeyed for position between lanes. Soon they were locked into an endless stream of red lights traveling at a lumbering pace. Once they passed the two-car accident up ahead, traffic began to thin out.

The entrance to the Rivercrest Square Shopping Center was bustling with activity. Patrons were dashing in and out of the Bourbon Street Grill; teenagers hung out in front of the Landmark Cinema; and a big, blue, furry mascot stood outside of Dick's Sporting Goods, directing potential customers his way.

Nikki continued to drive down the strip, past Claire's Fashion Jewelry and AT&T Wireless. "What exactly are we looking for?" she asked.

"Anything out of the ordinary."

"That's a pretty broad category. Care to narrow that down a bit?"

"Keep moving," Tony said, maintaining a serious look. "I'll know it when I see it."

"Sounds like pornography," she said with a laugh.

"Huh?"

"You know, porn."

"Yeah," Tony replied, tilting his head toward her. "I know porn."

"Well, few people can define it, but nobody has trouble pointing it out."

Tony rolled his eyes. "Drive."

Nikki made several more slow passes down the strip. "This is insane. We don't know who or what we're supposed to be looking for."

"Keep driving," Tony ordered.

"This is our fifth pass." *And you're driving me crazy,* she thought.

"I'm aware of that. Make another run."

Nikki gritted her teeth. "All right."

Another ten minutes of aimless cruising passed by.

"Over there," Tony shouted, pointing to the right.

"Where?"

"Up ahead, outside patio, Bourbon Street Grill."

Nikki pulled up next to the curb. Tony jumped out.

"Hey," she yelled. "Where..."

Tony was gone, halfway across the promenade. Nikki hit the hazard lights on the center console and engaged the electronic parking brake. She rushed out of the car and followed him.

The commotion gained the attention of an anchor-bearded man dining at the grill. He recognized Tony and stood up.

"Don't make me chase you," Tony hollered from a distance.

The man paused for a moment, patted himself down as if he'd misplaced something in his blazer, then leaped over the patio gates and sprinted toward Dick's Sporting Goods.

MATT LEATHERWOOD JR.

Tony ran after him. Nikki lingered behind, just in case he doubled back. The man picked up speed, rounded a commercial trash bin, and headed for the parking lot. Tony adjusted, gaining ground. Seconds later, he managed to close the distance to a single arm's length. Tony threw himself into the air and drove his shoulder into the man's back. The force propelled the stranger face-first onto the pavement. A small crowd quickly gathered. "Kick his ass!" one bystander shouted. "Bring the pain!" yelled another.

Tony wrestled the man onto his side. "Didn't I tell you not to run?"

He squirmed underneath him. "Please don't hurt me," he pleaded.

Tony eased up a bit, shifting his bodyweight.

"You're not Patrone," the man said.

"What gave it away, my Caucasian-Asian features?"

"Patrone said not to trust anybody but him. Where's Mr. Patrone?"

At that moment, Nikki arrived on the scene. "What the hell's going on?" she asked, out of breath.

Tony turned toward her and smiled. "Our friend here appears to be waiting on Patrone."

Nikki's eyes shot up. "Really?"

"Patrone," the bearded man repeated. "Where's Mr. Patrone?"

Tony grabbed him by his blazer lapels and yanked him up slightly off the ground. "If I knew, I wouldn't be manhandling you. So listen to me very carefully. I'm going to release my hold on you, you're going to stand, and the three of us are going to converse with each other like adults. Understand?"

The man nodded eagerly. Once the action had died down, the small crowd dispersed.

"What's your name?" Nikki asked once he was on his feet.

The man wrinkled his brow as if he were in deep concentration. "Clayton Thomas Austern."

"Profession?"

"He's an accountant," Tony chimed in.

Nikki paused at Tony's revelation and turned to look over at him.

"Let me bring you up to speed, Frank," Tony began. "Austern here was a bean counter hired by my boss to review our books for an upcoming internal audit."

Nikki was intrigued. "Is that true?"

"Yes," Austern said. "I first came into contact with Mr. Patrone on Mr. Quinn's yacht. He approached me and my assistant, Priscilla, while we were working."

"What did he want?"

Austern hesitated. His cheeks reddened, and he looked away.

"Well?" Nikki pressed.

"Forgive me, miss," he cautioned, "but, um, sexual relations with Priscilla."

"That's it?" Tony complained.

"Well, no."

Nikki touched Austern's elbow lightly. "What else, Clayton?"

He glanced back over at her. "He handed us his business card, so I contacted him a day or two later to follow up."

"Now we're getting somewhere," Tony said, slapping the accountant across the back. "Go on."

"Mr. Patrone mentioned he'd be coming into a large sum of money soon and wanted to know if I could move it for him undetected to an offshore account."

"Where?" Nikki asked.

"He never told me. That's what today's meeting was about. Mr. Patrone was going to fill in all the blanks, and I was going to give him a firm quote for my services."

"When were you supposed to meet?"

Austern glanced at his Frederique Constant watch. "About half an hour ago."

"Okay," Tony cut in. "Here's what were gonna do. Austern, you're gonna park your rear end at a table back at the Bourbon Street Grill. And Frank?"

Nikki perked up.

"You and I are gonna get back in the car and watch from a distance. There's a chance Patrone might still show up. Clayton?"

"Yes, sir."

"Don't screw this up, or I'll cut your balls off and waterboard you with all the blood pouring out of you."

CHAPTER TWENTY-FIVE

T wo more hours passed: still no Patrone. Nikki pointed to the clock on the dashboard. "It's late. Do you want to call it, Chen?"

Tony frowned. "Might as well."

"And Clayton?"

"I'll flip you for it. Loser makes the long trek over to the Bourbon Street Grill to tell him he can go."

Nikki flashed him a halfhearted smile. "Sure. Why not?"

Tony removed the double-tailed quarter from his pants pocket, tossed it into the air, and caught it. "Call it?"

"Tails," Nikki replied.

Tony kept the coin covered. "You sure?"

"Yeah, tails."

"Okay, it's your funeral." Tony's cell phone rang. "I gotta take this," he said, placing the coin back in his pocket.

Nikki's face tightened. *How convenient.*

The phone rang again.

"You gonna answer that?"

Tony glanced at the screen and swiped his finger across it to accept the call. "Chen here."

"Chen, it's Bosky. I got a BOLO hit on Patrone's Mercedes."

"Great. Where?"

"Coral Point Harbor, near the marina's long-term parking lot."

"Got it."

"And Chen?" Bosky cautioned.

"Yeah."

"Better hurry if you want first dibs on the wheels. The lead investigator was just dispatched."

"Roger."

"Patrone has crossed the line," Bosky reminded him. "He needs to be dealt with, and that's outside of the criminal justice system."

"Agreed."

Nikki raised her eyebrows in silent question.

"Head to Coral Point Harbor," Tony said. "And step on it."

"What about Austern?"

Tony chuckled. "He'll figure it out, eventually. Besides, Bosky told me Patrone's car just popped up near the marina's long-term parking lot. We gotta get there before the cops do."

Nikki fired up the Buick and roared out of the parking lot. Traffic leading away from the shopping center was sparse. Nikki continued to speed down the thoroughfare before turning off Rivercrest Road onto Dalton Highway.

"Pull in over there for a minute," Tony said, pointing to the right.

"Where?"

"That shopping plaza."

"Why?" Nikki asked, surprised at his request.

"Simply follow the instructions I give you."

Nikki cut across two lanes, hit the right blinker, and slowed down before turning into the square.

"Head over to that dollar store," Tony directed.

"A dollar store?"

"Just do it," he insisted. "Got it?"

Nikki pulled up next to the curb. The distinct roar of the Buick's turbocharged engine transitioned into plethora of low, grumbling exhaust notes.

Tony removed his wallet from inside his charcoal jacket. "Keep it running."

"Oh, no! You are *not* about to turn this into a Lifetime movie."

Tony shot her an annoyed look.

She placed the vehicle in park. "Too many women are sitting in the pen right now because somebody said, 'keep it running.'"

Tony unfastened his seat belt and got out of the car. "Suit yourself."

Nikki jumped out right behind him. "I most certainly will."

The two rushed inside the building. The store's recent renovations featured a fresh interior paint job, a new halogen lighting system, and the addition of several new wall coolers up front, near the registers. Tony quickly moved up and down the aisles, working his way from the front of the store to the back. Nikki was right behind him when he stopped abruptly in household cleaning supplies and tossed her a pack of disposable latex gloves. She jumped back, fumbling to catch the item. Tony continued on, darting past health and beauty products then party supplies. Finally, he reached the far corner of the store, where he scanned through the products hanging from the shelves. Nothing. He then rummaged past several packs of action figures, die-cast model cars, and air pistols.

"Toys?" Nikki questioned.

"Yep."

She rolled her eyes. *Unbelievable.*

Tony rummaged around some more then suddenly stopped. "Got it," he announced, holding up a plastic package with a purple cardboard insert.

Nikki looked up at the item then smiled. "Oh, you're good."

CHAPTER TWENTY-SIX

Tony fumbled around with the plastic package while Nikki drove. Inside, affixed to the purple cardboard insert, was a metallic police detective badge mounted on a faux-leather backing. Tony removed the item and held it in his hand. "This should do the trick."

"But can you sell it?" Nikki asked.

"That depends…"

Nikki pulled up to the Coral Point Harbor entrance and stopped next to the large brown-and-white sign identifying the area. She glanced at Tony. "Depends on what?"

"How fast you get me there. If the lead investigator is already on the scene, then we're SOL."

Nikki hit the accelerator, throwing Tony back in his seat. He cursed over the quick burst of speed. "Sheesh, you could've warned me, Frank."

"Yep, I could've," Nikki said with a laugh, "but it wouldn't have been as much fun. Your reaction was priceless."

"Glad I could entertain you."

She continued to race down the winding road toward the water, where numerous boats were restrained to piers spaced out across the horizon. A briny fish-and-sea-grass odor filtered through the Buick's AC vents.

Tony sniffed the air and made a strange face. "Is your window cracked?"

"No."

"Smells like you need a new air filter."

"I just had this vehicle serviced," Nikki lied, knowing full well she'd only had the car for a couple of weeks.

"Well, don't take it back to the same place."

The winding road opened into a sunlit clearing. Gentle waves rippled across the water like a finger over the keys of a piano.

"It's really quite simple," Tony commented. "Take a Torx number twenty-five screwdriver, remove the plastic covering, and disconnect the two intake hoses. Next, unbuckle the clamps on each side of the air-filter housing group and swap out the stock filter."

"Noted," Nikki said. "I'll get right on it."

Tony stared at her, annoyed.

Nikki shrugged. "Just sayin'."

Tony reached down and pulled the pack of latex gloves from the shopping bag and opened it. Nikki glanced over to see what he was doing. Tony took the gloves out, paired them together in sets, then rolled each pair into a separate ball before shoving them all inside his jacket.

When they arrived at the clearing's end, he pointed toward a building two hundred yards away, to the left. "Over there," he said.

"I can see the harbor office just fine," Nikki replied.

"Not the harbor office. *Behind it.*"

Nikki refocused her attention on the area in question. Flashing blue lights emanated in a consistent, rhythmic pattern from a parking lot just beyond the structure. "Got it."

Tony reached up and adjusted the rearview mirror a bit before playing around with his hair.

Nikki drove past the harbor office toward the parking lot. "Role prep?"

"Gotta feel the part," Tony said, adjusting his jacket while shaking his shoulders.

"I suppose you're gonna need some gum to add to the stereotype?"

Tony shrugged. "Wouldn't hurt."

"Cup holder," Nikki directed.

Tony reached down, grabbed a stick of Orbit gum, unwrapped it, and popped it into his mouth. A slight smile tugged at the corners of his lips as he began to chew. "Let me do all the talking."

Nikki eased the sedan to a complete stop and engaged the electric parking brake. "Sure thing."

"Relax," Tony said, fumbling with the phony badge in his hand. "I got this."

Nikki forced a perfunctory smile. *This is a disaster waiting to happen.*

The two got out of the vehicle and approached the harbor patrol officer standing next to his cruiser. He was short and muscular, with russet-colored hair that was receding. In the distance was a silver Mercedes Roadster, erratically parked, with the silhouette of a body behind the wheel.

"What do we have here?" Tony asked.

The patrolman looked up from his electronic tablet and frowned. A strong chin protruded from his wide jawline. "And you two are?"

"Detectives Chen and Frank," Tony replied, quickly flipping his phony badge. "Criminal Investigation Division."

"You got here rather quickly."

"A fast driver helps."

The patrolman stared at the severely damaged sedan they'd just pulled up in as his siren lights continued to flash electric blue. "Didn't know they issued beater cars to detectives in the CID."

"They don't," Nikki chimed in. "We're working a joint venture with narcotics and some of their undercovers."

The patrolman pursed his lips but didn't say anything.

Tony continued chewing his gum while he met the officer's stare. His body tightened. "Incident report?" he asked again.

The patrolman pointed to the silver Roadster several yards away. "I came across that vehicle while patrolling my regular beat."

Nikki noticed the Mercedes was parked in the center of the lot's travel lane, facing against traffic.

"I ran the plates," he continued. "Popped up on a recent BOLO, so I called it in." The officer glanced back down at his tablet; the battery was almost dead. "The vehicle belongs to a Victor Patrone, whom I assume is the stiff behind the wheel."

Tony looked surprised. "Thanks. We'll take a closer look now."

"Knock yourself out. I'm gonna go charge this thing back up," the patrolman said, holding up his tablet, "then call for a bus and a coroner."

Tony nodded. "Frank, you take the passenger side," he ordered, motioning for her to move in that direction. "I'll take the driver's side."

Cautiously they approached the Mercedes. Tony reached inside his jacket and tossed Nikki a set of the gloves he'd prepared earlier. "Use these," he directed. She caught them and put them on. Upon closer inspection, the pair realized the silhouette was clearly that of a deceased male.

"It's Patrone," Tony announced, peering through the driver's-side window. "Looks like two shots, close range."

He put on a pair of gloves and pulled open the car door. The dome light came on. Blood was splattered all over the upholstery. "Damn, what a fucking mess."

Nikki shook her head then popped open the passenger door. She leaned inside the cab and checked Patrone's neck for a carotid pulse. "He's definitely dead. Scratch marks around the face suggest a struggle."

"Well, it was only a matter of time. Whether I got to him or someone else did, the outcome would've been the same."

Nikki scanned the body then performed a quick pat down of Patrone's jacket. "We've got a missing sidearm, Chen. Empty holster."

"Anything else?"

She looked around. "Keys seem to be missing. Some travel pamphlets and a scarf are on the floorboard."

"Grab 'em."

Nikki scooped up the items and circled back around the Roadster to the driver's side. "Looks like travel plans to Costa Rica," she said, handing Tony the brochures.

"Interesting...and the scarf?"

She held it up. "I'll be damned."

Tony's eyebrows rose. "What?"

"Roberto Cavalli."

"Who?"

"It's a one-of-a-kind floral print," Nikki explained. "By a world-renowned Italian fashion designer."

Tony looked unimpressed. "What's that got to do with the business at hand?"

"Everything, because it tells me that Lacey was with Patrone."

"Oh, really?" Now he looked interested.

"Yeah, she purchased this hideous neckwear earlier today."

"That explains the 'where to' and the 'who,' but..." Tony paused and hit the trunk's release switch. "Where's the money?"

An audible click sounded as the top of the trunk lifted. The two of them moved to the back of the car. Tony raised the trunk open. "Bingo."

Nikki looked inside. At the bottom of the trunk was an open duffel bag filled with money. It looked exactly like the one

Spence was carrying when they were raided. Her eyes locked on to a few of the hundred-dollar bills: they looked strange to her. A large quill hovered over an inkwell on the front of each note, and a large gold "100" was emblazoned on the back. "We're a bag short," she announced.

Tony nodded setting the travel brochures and scarf down inside the trunk. "You caught that too?"

"Yeah." *And the treasury must have redesigned the currency while I was locked up*, she thought.

"Whenever we collect our street money for the quarter," Tony explained, "we always split the revenue and place it into two separate duffel bags."

Nikki leaned forward and attempted to pick up the bag with both hands. "Damn," she said. "That's heavy."

Tony grinned. "Seventy-five pounds."

Nikki stood back up. "And I felt everyone last one of them."

He shrugged. "Cash is heavy."

Nikki knew this to be true through task force cross-training with the Secret Service. Used paper currency was 25 percent linen and 75 percent cotton. Through massive circulation, it got heavier due to the absorption of oil, dirt, and moisture, adding as much as another twenty-five percent to its base weight.

Nikki shook her shoulders to loosen them up. "My guess is Lacey killed Patrone, grabbed what she could carry, and hightailed it outta here."

"Agreed," Tony said, in between smacks of his gum. "Definitely working alone. If she had a partner, they'd have taken both bags."

CHAPTER TWENTY-SEVEN

"Detectives," the patrolman called out as he approached Nikki and Tony.

Tony closed the trunk and spun around.

"Yes," Nikki replied, stepping forward to cut the officer off.

The patrolman stopped a few feet in front of her. "The bus is on its way, but the coroner will be delayed. She's working a double homicide on the east side of town."

"Good to know. Thanks."

"You two discover anything new?"

Nikki shook her head. "Just a few travel brochures on the floorboard. Other than that, nothing. Forensics will have to scour this vehicle from top to bottom to find any decent leads."

"Brochures," the officer repeated, crossing his arms. "Where to?"

Nikki removed her gloves. "Costa Rica."

He stroked his chin and frowned. "Hmm."

An audible click from inside the Mercedes sounded. Everyone's attention shifted to the trunk as it popped open, exposing the duffel bag filled with money. Tony exchanged a nervous glance with Nikki.

"Whoa," the patrolman said, releasing the holster-retention strap on his service weapon.

The hairs on the back of Nikki's neck stood up. "Looks like drug money."

"I think you might be right, Dee-tec-tive."

A stranger wearing an orange neoprene life jacket and an Atlanta Braves baseball cap approached the group from behind.

Tony and the patrol officer drew their firearms instantly.

The man raised his hands, revealing the vehicle's smart key in his possession. "That's my money in there."

The patrolman shifted his gaze between Tony and the stranger. "What the hell's going on?"

"All right, everybody just calm down here," Nikki said, attempting to defuse the situation. "Who are you and what are you doing with that smart key?"

"Just a simple boat pilot, ma'am, here to collect what's rightfully mine."

Tony spat out the gum in his mouth and curled his lips into a small grin. "And what makes you think the contents of that trunk belong to you?"

"Because I have this," the man replied, holding out the smart key to the Mercedes. "Possession is nine-tenths of the law. Right, Officer?"

The patrolman rolled his eyes. "Not when it comes to drug money."

"That's your assertion, not a proven fact. The money in that trunk is mine. It belongs to me."

"Arrest him," Tony ordered, tucking his P239 back inside his waistband behind his back.

The patrolman approached the boat pilot with his weapon drawn. "Hands behind your back."

"Whoa, for what?"

"Put your hands behind your back, sir," the officer commanded again.

The boat pilot slowly lowered his hands and placed them behind his back. "What's happening?"

"I'm restraining you for your safety and mine, at least until we get this situation sorted out."

"My safety?" the pilot questioned. "But you're the one with the gun."

The patrolman holstered his weapon and placed one cuff around the pilot's wrist. "Don't resist."

"I'm not resisting."

"Good," the officer said, placing the second cuff on. "Then neither of us will get hurt here."

Nikki walked over to the man and stared him down. His face was riddled with rosacea. "Now, about this drug money—"

"Lady, I don't know anything about no drug money. All I know is that a blonde with a killer rack just paid me five thousand dollars to take her to Slip Island."

Everyone's eyes widened.

"Go ahead," the pilot urged. "Check my jacket pockets."

The patrolman frisked the mariner. Inside the windbreaker he wore beneath his life jacket were two $2,500 stacks of cash.

"See? I told you," the pilot said. "I'm the victim here."

The patrolman rolled his eyes again. "Right, buddy. More like the opportunist."

"How long has it been since you made that run to Slip Island?" Nikki asked.

"Forty-five minutes. Miss Silicone titties tossed me the cash. I dropped her off, and then she gave me the smart key and told me there was even more in the trunk of an abandoned Mercedes back at the marina."

"Oh, this just keeps getting better and better," the officer replied. "Wouldn't you say, Dee-tec-tives?"

An eerie feeling swept over Nikki, a foreboding sense that the patrolman wasn't buying their charade. A tingling sensation ran up and down her spine, like the poll numbers of a politician caught in a sex scandal days before an election.

The officer drew his service weapon and pointed it at them. "Now who did you say you dee-tec-tives report to at CID?"

Tony's mouth fell open. "Lieutenant Bosky," he said quickly.

The officer chuckled. "Since when does CID report to narcotics?"

"Joint venture," Nikki cut in. "I thought we established that when we first arrived."

"I don't know what's going on here, but my gut tells me something's up. I'm calling it in."

"Could I have a word with my partner in private?" Tony asked.

"You do what you gotta do, Dee-tec-tive. Headquarters will have this whole thing sorted out within the hour."

Tony grabbed Nikki by the arm and pulled her to the side. "Look," he said, whispering, "Lacey has a forty-five-minute to an hour head start. Find her and the rest of my boss's cash."

"What are you going to do?" Nikki asked.

"Whatever it takes to clear things up with Barney Fife here. I can't take the risk of having half my boss's money seized and placed in an evidence locker room somewhere."

"Understood."

"And Frank?"

"Yeah."

"Don't get any ideas about disappearing with the rest of the cash. It would be a shame if I had to turn around and hunt you down as well."

Nikki raised her hands up in a surrender gesture. "That won't be necessary. I don't want any trouble here."

"Excellent. Then I suggest you get moving."

Nikki slowly backed away from Tony with her hands still up.

The patrolman quickly trained his gun on her. "Where're you going?"

Nikki didn't say a word.

"She's going after the suspect," Tony answered. "You know, the one our handcuffed friend here said paid him off and gave him the smart key to the Mercedes."

"I don't think that's a good idea, Dee-tec-tive."

Tony shook his head. "Oh, but obstructing justice and aiding and abetting a criminal is?"

The patrolman smirked at Tony's suggestion.

"I promise you," Tony continued, "if this investigation is a bust, when the department is finally done sorting this out, I'll personally see to it that you can't even get hired in this town as a rent-a-cop."

The officer hesitated for a moment then motioned with his gun for Nikki to flee. "Go, before I change my mind."

Nikki lowered her hands as she continued to walk backward. When she was out of the patrolman's line of fire, she turned around and disappeared into the coastal landscape.

CHAPTER TWENTY-EIGHT

The *Sea Coach Express* approached the dock slowly from its port side. Nikki waited until the small passenger boat came to a complete stop before she boarded with the rest of the passengers. It had been nearly impossible for her to find a trip pilot willing to run her up to Slip Island for a fair price on such short notice, so she settled for a tourist water taxi.

The tour guide wore khaki pants, a short-sleeve white shirt, and a life jacket. She also donned a yacht captain's hat and pair of round-framed Ray-Bans. "My name's Jenny Dillon," she announced in a Southern drawl, handing out dry bags to each of the passengers for their personal belongings. "I'll be guiding you along the Slip Island Coast, through the various pirate ruins, to the main island and ultimately to Captain Sidney 'Cutthroat' Scott's stronghold."

Nikki placed her phone along with her wristlet inside the bag then put on the life jacket she found resting on her seat. She glanced around. The thirty-seat craft was full. Most of the people were tourists, wearing sun hats, floral-print shirts, cargo shorts, and sandals.

Once everyone was seated, the pilot eased out into the water.

"Captain Scott," Jenny continued, "was a nineteenth-century English sea captain, most noted for preying on ships off the

Carolina coast then hightailing it down to Georgia to evade capture. Slip Island was Captain Scott's main base of operation. Its name is derived from the raider's unique ability to give the US Navy the slip while—"

"Everybody hold on," the pilot warned as he pushed the throttle forward.

Nikki gripped the seat in front of her. The wind picked up, shearing through her hair and sending sea spray flying into her face. Instinctively she tucked her chin to her chest and held her head down low.

The *Sea Coach Express* quickly accelerated to thirty-one knots then dropped back down to twenty-three before leveling off. It took a moment for everyone to adjust to the variance. The endless jarring of the boat plowing through waves at a high rate of speed left some passengers feeling woozy.

Upon the boat's approach, Nikki spotted Slip Island emerging from the abyss and breaking the line of the deep-blue horizon.

Jenny removed her hand from the steel canopy bar she used to brace herself and pointed out the brick ruins of a fort nestled on a bluff that overlooked the water. "Over to my left, high above, you can see the remains of one of Captain Scott's interim fortifications. This fortress successfully kept authorities at bay, until his main stronghold farther inland could be constructed."

Several tourists, seated on the starboard side of the craft, rushed over to the port side to take a look. Nikki gritted her teeth, suppressing the urge to scream, as people surrounded her. A large, sweaty man encroaching on her personal space tossed red warning flags throughout her mind. In prison, such an intimate violation would get you killed or, at the very least, seriously maimed. However, this wasn't prison, and the responses of that world were no longer acceptable in mainstream society.

Nikki took a deep breath then exhaled. *Relax. He's not a threat*, she told herself. Another breath followed. *You're safe.* She repeated those words to herself a couple more times until she calmed down.

A few minutes later, everyone was directed back to their seats. Nikki let out a sigh of relief.

"Eventually," Jenny continued, picking up where she'd left off, "the US Navy apprehended Captain Scott, tried and convicted him of piracy on the high seas, then sentenced him to death by hanging. On July fourth, 1826, that judgment was carried out. At Captain Scott's own request, he was strung up from the mainmast of his ship, *Poseidon's Plague*."

Nikki raised her eyebrows in interest.

"During the Civil War," Jenny continued, "Slip Island became home to freed slaves and was a site for schools taught by prominent abolitionists. After the war, it became a fueling station for the navy. Marines soon arrived to provide security for the new military installation. By World War I, Slip Island had become a forward deployment site for troops bound for the European front, and it remained as such until the end of World War II."

The *Sea Coach Express* motored passed three small skerries that formed a chain and converged into a long white ribbon of sand that led to the main island. Nikki noticed a few more water taxis up ahead, approaching an extended modular dock. The *Sea Coach* cut across the water at an angle and into the dissipating wake of the other crafts.

"Today, Slip Island is on the National Register of Historic Places maintained by the National Park Service and is a favorite destination of Peach State tourists, as y'all will soon find out."

The water taxi pulled up to the dock and was quickly tied off by the shore party.

"Ladies and gentlemen, please gather your belongings," Jenny announced. "This includes children and significant others."

A few passengers burst into laughter.

"We'll meet over by Randall's Bait and Gift Shop, so please stay together."

The passengers disembarked in an orderly fashion and made their way up the aluminum gangway to the cement pier. Nikki lingered behind on purpose, hoping to separate herself from the group.

"Stay together," Jenny reminded everyone, as the group extended and contracted like an accordion.

Nikki removed her phone from her dry bag and called the lifeline.

The phone rang once and was answered immediately. "Touch of Style Salon, Janice speaking. How may I help you?"

"Agent 2294," Nikki said. "Day code, business section, September seventeenth, identification procedure."

"Proceed."

"Consultant, transparency, merger."

Janice took a few moments to verify the words. "Confirmed. What's going on, Cousin Nikki?"

"Patrone is dead. Local PD put out a BOLO for his vehicle and got a hit down by the harbor. Suspect was found slumped behind the wheel—two shots, close range. Inside his trunk was a duffel bag with 1.25 million in drug money to be laundered up to New York. All preliminary evidence at the scene points to Lacey Johnson, an associate of Gemini Cordoza, as the perpetrator."

"Noted."

"Perp is believed to have fled to Slip Island. I'm currently in pursuit."

"How can I help with your search?" Janice asked.

"Query the system for all possible locations where Lacey could have fled to. We're dealing with a woman in her early thirties, in moderate to good shape, hauling approximately seventy-five pounds of bundled cash in a duffel bag. She's got to be exhausted, in a frantic mind-set, armed, and potentially dangerous."

"Stand by."

Nikki waited while Janice conducted the search.

"Got it," she announced several minutes later. "Birch Field."

"What's that?"

"A private airport, originally established by the federal government shortly after World War I. Deactivated in the nineties and deeded back to the island. Covers three hundred seventy-three acres, with two asphalt runways. Houses twenty-six single-engine planes and two multiengine aircraft."

"Location?"

"Based on your cell-phone coordinates, exactly eleven miles from your current position. I'm dispatching a chase team as backup." Two back-to-back alert tones interrupted the conversation. "Hold on," Janice said, then returned a minute or two later. "Cousin Nikki, are you there?"

"Yes. What's going on?"

"Emergency break in the line. Harlan is patching through."

"Nicole?"

"Yes, Harlan."

"Janice brought me up to speed on your situation. If at all possible, the Crime Enforcement Task Force needs Lacey to be brought in without incident. This is our collar."

"Understood."

"She's the linchpin that can testify that the money in question was drug money that Patrone was delivering on behalf of Quinn to be laundered to cartel leadership out of state. Without her, all we've got is a dead guy dropping off lots of cash but deciding at the last minute to keep it for himself."

"Anything else?"

"The K-9 team has picked up a positive scent trail on your brother. They're following it as we speak."

Nikki's face lit up. "Where?"

"Wooded area, a mile and a half from Paris Oaks."

"That's a bit far from campus, isn't it?"

"Not according to the lead handler. Depending on conditions, human scent from a walking subject could easily travel hundreds of yards or more. Throw in little to no vegetation, heat radiating off concrete, the wind, and the melting pot of aromas intermingling in the middle of downtown Parkbridge, and we're very fortunate to get a lead like this early on."

"Exceptionally fortunate. I just won't have peace of mind until Marty is found."

"I'm on top of this, Nicole. Just stay focused."

"I am, but it's taking everything I've got just to hold it together. Sometimes I just want to scream."

"So do it," Harlan urged.

"What?"

"Scream."

"Now?"

"Yes."

Nikki looked around. Most of the tour group had gathered at Randall's Bait and Gift Shop. She quickly covered the phone's speaker and screamed as loudly as she could. The piercing sound startled the tourists, several of whom turned in her direction to see what the commotion was all about.

"Sorry, just found out I'm pregnant," Nikki lied.

Scattering praise and shouts of congratulations emanated from the crowd.

Nikki waved, acknowledging them, then got back on the phone.

"Now how do you feel?" Harlan asked.

"Much better."

"Good. We're almost across the finish line. Stay the course."

"Harlan…"

"Yes?"

"Thanks." Nikki hung up before he could respond. She

placed her phone inside her wristlet, discarded the dry bag, then climbed up the gangway to the pier.

A handful of tourists were staring at Nikki, their faces smeared with curiosity. She ignored them as she walked past the bait and gift shop toward a group of cabs lined up at an adjacent taxi stand.

"Everything okay?" Jenny shouted.

Nikki whirled around. "Yes, I just really need to find the guy I've been sleeping with."

"Handle your business, girl, but don't be surprised if turns out not to be worth the hassle."

Nikki forced a smile and got inside the first cab. The driver glanced at her in the rearview mirror. "Where to?"

"Birch Field."

"Birch Field it is," the driver said, hitting the meter. "Business or pleasure?"

Nikki reached underneath her oversize shirt and removed a Glock 27 subcompact pistol concealed within a body holster that also functioned as ladies' shapewear. "Business."

"Look, I don't want no trouble here," he pleaded, watching her in the rearview.

The cab swerved into the opposite lane, nearly sideswiping an orange pickup truck.

"Pay attention to the road," Nikki yelled.

The driver diverted his attention away from the mirror and regained control of the cab.

Nikki reached inside the pocket on the opposite side of her body holster, removed her official wallet badge, and held it up. "Special Agent Nicole Frank. Relax."

"Oh, oh, okay. Sorry."

Nikki placed her credentials back inside her holster.

The driver chuckled.

"Something funny?"

"Yeah, you identified yourself as a federal agent then told me to relax, as opposed to saying, 'Federal agent…you're under arrest.' That's oxymoronic."

Nikki smiled. "We don't utter that phrase very often, so count your blessings."

The driver didn't reply but kept an eye on her in the mirror while he continued to drive.

Nikki released the magazine from the semiautomatic and placed it on her lap. Pointing the handgun away from the driver, she racked the slide back. He jumped.

"Chill," she said, retrieving the chambered round. "Just a routine equipment check before I take a suspect into custody."

The driver perked up a little. "Oh."

Nikki emptied the rounds in her magazine and reloaded them. When she finished, she inserted the magazine back into the semiautomatic and racked the slide a second time to chamber a round. This time the driver smiled widely.

"Is the situation serious?" he asked.

"Always."

"What did he do?"

"It's a she," Nikki corrected. "Possible murder suspect."

"Oh."

"You sound surprised."

The driver shook his head. "I am. What's this world coming to?"

"It's a cold, dark place out there," Nikki said. "And everyone's doing whatever they can to get over on somebody else, and sometimes that leads to murder. We might not like it, but we damn sure have to deal with it."

"Better you than me."

Nikki reholstered her weapon. "Point taken."

The driver drove swiftly through the tourist town, taking the less-traveled roads. When he saw traffic congestion or pedestrian activity, he changed course. Fifteen minutes later, they arrived at the airport's main terminal.

"Here you are, Birch Field," the driver announced.

Nikki removed her phone from her wristlet and clipped it to her side then pulled out her driver's license and credit card, leaving only cash inside the small purse.

"And might I add," the driver said, smiling at her in the rearview mirror, "I got you here ten minutes faster than it would normally take, ma'am."

Nikki checked the price on the meter then tossed him her pocketbook. "Thanks, everything inside is yours."

He caught it and quickly thumbed through it to verify the amount. "Good luck catching your criminal."

Nikki exited the vehicle then dashed through the terminal doors, quickly scanning the small waiting area for Lacey. She noticed her right away, clutching a zipped-up duffel bag and talking to a member of the flight crew. When Lacey's eyes caught Nikki's, she scowled. Nikki approached her with caution, questions forming in her mind. "We need to talk," she told Lacey.

Lacey moved in the opposite direction. "No, we don't."

"Lacey," Nikki admonished. "I'm here to help."

The gap between them extended.

"Gemini send you?"

"No."

Lacey eyed Nikki with increased suspicion. The muscles in her face tightened. "I find that hard to believe, very hard to believe."

"Well, he didn't." Nikki shrugged and made a wry little face. "He has no idea I'm here."

Lacey picked up her pace.

"Don't make me chase you," Nikki warned.

Lacey kept moving then made a break at the last second for a long hallway at the back of the waiting area.

"Damn it, Lacey." *I hate it when they run*, she thought. Nikki shook her head and took off after her.

A mixed crowd of men and women fled from the corridor.

"Blondie's got a gun!" a businessman yelled.

The warning quickly rippled out the mouths of several others, accompanied by a chorus of screams from fellow passengers.

"Federal Agent," Nikki announced, drawing her weapon and moving past the commotion.

"In the ladies' room!" an elderly woman called out.

Nikki eased up next to the door from the push-plate side.

"Be careful, young lady."

Nikki acknowledged the woman with a nod, took a deep breath, and pushed the door open hard.

CHAPTER TWENTY-NINE

L acy had stuffed the sinks full of paper towels and turned all the faucets on high, hoping they might overflow before Nikki arrived. She then grabbed the nearby janitor's cart and dragged it behind her. Steam fogged the mirrors as water began to pour onto the floor.

The door burst open. Nikki charged in. "Special Agent Frank," she yelled, pushing through the kill zone.

Lacey flinched, letting go of the cart.

"Put your weapon down."

Lacey ignored the command and retreated to a midlevel window past the stalls. Frantic, she fumbled around for the sash lock, trying to open it.

"Put your weapon down now," Nikki ordered her.

Lacey chuckled as she turned around. "I knew you were too good to be true. Pork has a certain stench."

For a tense few seconds, the women stared each other down, ready to shoot.

Nikki pressed forward past the janitor's cart, watching Lacey like a jackal waiting to scavenge a fresh carcass. "Don't make this any harder than it has to be."

"And rob you of this golden opportunity to square off with me?"

Nikki came to within striking distance. "As much as I'd love to kick your ass, this is gonna go down by the book."

Lacey dropped the duffel bag on the floor, knelt, and placed the semiautomatic in front of her. "Pussy!"

Nikki moved in to kick the weapon away. Her phone rang. She hesitated. Lacey lunged forward, grabbing Nikki's leg and sweeping her off her feet. Nikki tumbled backward, hitting the floor hard and crying out in pain. Her Glock flew out of her hand and slid under one of the stalls. Lacey scrambled on top of her. The two women rolled around the wet floor, a blur of hands and feet. Nikki managed to pull one arm free and reached for the plastic caution: wet floor sign on the janitor's cart. She grabbed it and struck Lacey across the back repeatedly. Lacey let go of Nikki and flailed about. Nikki gasped for air, her heart racing. Exhausted, she yanked Lacey up from the floor and threw a solid punch across her face. The impact sent Lacey plummeting back to the floor.

Nikki rolled her over onto her stomach. "Lacey Johnson," she said, out of breath, "you're under arrest for the murder of Victor Patrone." She reached down and began to place Lacey's hands behind her back when her phone rang once again.

"Frank," she answered.

"Touch of Style—"

"Janice," Nikki said, cutting her off. "The suspect has been detained. Where's that chase team?"

"I just spoke with the team leader," Janice replied. "They're closing in on you now. Stand by. I've got Harlan on a separate line."

Nikki waited for Harlan to be patched through.

"Nicole, we found him. He's fine," Harlan announced.

"Marty?"

"Yes."

"What?" Nikki practically shrieked.

"Yeah, we're getting reports now that your brother was located in the woods, three and a half miles from Paris Oaks," Harlan replied.

"How'd he get there?"

"The rescue coordination specialist stated that the mentally disabled often get lost because they have no goal or intention beyond leaving their current location. They just go, like a car without a driver, until they get stuck by terrain or insurmountable obstacles."

Nikki reached underneath her wet shirt and removed a pair of zip-tie cuffs from her body holster. "What was Marty trying to do?" she asked.

"Nobody knows for sure, but Ms. Daniel from Paris Oaks believes he was trying to reach you. Something about his obsessive-compulsive disorder being triggered after he claimed he spotted you on campus—along with the repeated denial of a reunion with you—driving the compulsion."

She sighed. "Makes sense."

"Marty was nervous but excited when they found him. He said he was hungry, but as I mentioned, he appears to be fine."

"When can I see him?"

"I'm working on that now."

Nikki's spirit soared. "Thank you, Harlan."

"I'll be in touch when I have that issue resolved," he said, then hung up.

Nikki put her phone away and glanced down at Lacey. She was sprawled out on the floor, moaning. Nikki grabbed her by the hair and pulled her head back. Lacey looked up, stunned. "Not a word about me being a federal agent," Nikki warned.

"Or what?" Lacey asked defiantly.

"Or I'll tell Gem that you and Patrone were lovers who were working together to set him up as the fall guy for the Lascano cartel's missing money."

Lacey remained silent.

Nikki gave her hair a slight tug in response.

"Ow!" Lacey screamed. "Bitch, that hurt."

"If option one isn't enough to get you killed, I'll dime you out to Patrone's people myself. Speaking as someone who just got out of the pen, cartels love making examples out of criminals behind bars: captive audience, captive prey."

"Deal," Lacey said instantly. "You've got a deal."

Nikki let go of her hair and cuffed her hands behind her back. "Damn right we've got a deal, because bitches get shit done."

CHAPTER THIRTY

Two days had passed since the staged DEA bust. The chase team came and went; Lacey was in custody; and Nikki had managed to retrieve her Buick from the harbor parking lot. Now she stood outside the Compound gate, waiting as instructed, with the recovered money.

A black Rolls-Royce Phantom limousine pulled up next to her and stopped. The rear tinted window lowered. "Get in," Tony ordered.

The passenger door flew open. Inside, across from the bodyguard, sat Quinn. Nikki picked up the duffel bag and handed it to Tony then climbed inside.

"I trust it's all there," he said.

Nikki nodded. "It always has been."

Tony smiled. "Good, then I won't need to count it."

The Phantom pulled away from the curb.

"Gentlemen," Nikki said, "it appears our business has concluded."

Quinn raised his hand. "Not so fast." He traced his thumb and forefinger down the sides of his goatee.

Nikki's stomach churned, uncertainty gripping her.

"And the thief?" Quinn asked.

"You mean Lacey?"

"Whoever."

"I let her go."

Quinn's demeanor changed as a frown unfolded beneath his goatee. "Let her go?"

"That's right," Nikki said, turning away from his probing gaze and glancing out the window. The Rolls-Royce circled the block.

"Why?"

"Because I'm not a hired gun. I'm a broker who specializes in white-collar crime."

Quinn's frown melted as he exchanged a look of concern with his bodyguard. Tony sat motionless, the duffel bag on his lap as he rolled his double-tailed coin across his knuckles. Quinn shifted his attention back to Nikki.

"It was my understanding that I was to help retrieve the money," she continued.

"True."

Nikki hesitated, aware that she might be pushing the boundaries here. "I'm confused. Patrone is dead, and you have your money. That's a wash."

Quinn motioned with his head for Tony to give the duffel bag back to Nikki. The bodyguard pocketed his coin and handed over the cash.

"Good point," Quinn said.

Nikki was puzzled by the gesture. She studied Quinn's face, trying to figure him out, but he remained expressionless. All she could do was wait for an explanation.

"Nothing's changed," he said in an irritated tone. "The Cordoza crew is still responsible for laundering this money up to New York...unless I hear from Francisco, and I have yet to have that conversation."

"Oh," Nikki said, surprised.

Quinn glanced at Tony. "Have you heard from Francisco?"

The bodyguard shook his head. "Negative, boss."

Nikki grinned. "Gem will be pleased to hear this. Thank you."

"Bottom line," Quinn added, "Patrone was my employee, my problem. His indiscretions shouldn't reflect negatively on you. If anything, it shows structural flaws within my organization, something I can't afford to make known at this time."

The Rolls-Royce approached the gated driveway of the Compound. The chauffeur paused for a moment to allow the groundskeeper to grant him access. Seconds later, the automated gate retracted into the frame. The Phantom pulled forward and headed straight toward the hotel. Once it arrived, the chauffeur stepped out of the limo and placed the two duffel bags next to each other on the curb.

Quinn lowered the passenger window to eye level. "We'll be in touch," he said.

Nikki gave him a cursory nod as the window rose back up. An instant later, the Rolls-Royce was gone.

Nikki stooped to pick up one of the duffel bags. She buckled beneath the weight of it as she staggered from the portico to the lobby entrance. The automated doors whisked opened. She stepped inside, dropped the bag on the floor, and pressed the intercom button on the wall. "Willard," Nikki called out. "Gemini!" No one responded. She pressed the button again and waited. Nothing.

"Hello? Anybody there?"

Finally, Willard appeared from around the corner.

"You sleeping on the job?" Nikki asked as he approached.

He shook his head. "I'm the consummate professional, Ms. Frank."

Nikki smirked at the remark.

"What can I do for you, ma'am?"

She pointed to the automated doors behind her. "One professional to another, could you grab that second duffel bag out on the curb and take it to the main conference suite?"

Willard nodded. "Will do."

"Thank you."

Cordoza arrived moments later, slightly out breath. "What's going on?"

Nikki's stomach tightened. "We need to talk."

Cordoza picked up the duffel bag next to her. "Clearly you salvaged the deal, so what's this about?"

The two moved forward.

"Lacey bailed on us," Nikki said flatly.

Cordoza stopped and dropped the bag. "I was afraid that might happen."

A long pause followed as he zoned out.

"Gem?"

"Yeah."

"I'm sorry this happened to you."

The vacant look on Cordoza's face began to dissipate. "Really, I should've known. She'd been acting strange the past couple of months," he admitted. "Cold, distant, secretive."

"Looks like present circumstances have only confirmed what you already knew to be true in your heart."

Cordoza nodded. "How long ago?"

"Several hours."

"Did she say where she was headed or why she was leaving?"

Nikki hesitated. "No, just that she needed space."

Cordoza chuckled. "Space? Really?"

"I know," Nikki replied. "It's one of those cryptic things we women say whenever we don't want to confront our issues head on."

Cordoza pulled in a deep breath and shook his head. "How convenient."

"Look, I know you're hurting, but these things take time."

Cordoza clenched his jaw tightly. "When in the hell has time ever solved anything?"

Nikki didn't answer.

"That's what I thought," Cordoza said, picking up the duffel bag at his side.

"Gem—"

"Enough. Let's get to work."

CHAPTER THIRTY-ONE

Nikki returned to the warehouse later that afternoon. Inside, it was warm and well lit by natural light. She made her way over to the modified shipping container and noticed the door was propped open this time. The makeshift office had been freshly painted to reflect the new ownership of the building.

Nikki stepped inside the container. Harlan and Special Agent Bolston sat next to each other on one side of the table. Director Kepler remained standing, leaning against the wall, perusing a newspaper.

"Everything is set in motion," Nikki announced. "Cordoza and I will launder the cash for Quinn by the agreed-upon deadline."

Kameko gave her a thumbs-up.

"Terrific work, Nicole," Harlan said, removing his glasses and wiping them clean.

Nikki smiled. "Thank you."

"Once you initiate the process," he continued, putting his glasses back on, "we'll sit tight, follow the digital footprints, and see where they lead."

"Hopefully they'll lead to something big," Director Kepler added. "There's a lot riding on this."

"Agreed," Kameko said.

Director Kepler folded his newspaper and placed it on the table. "Agent Frank…"

Nikki perked up.

"Personally, I didn't think you'd be able to salvage the deal. I was prepared to write this off as a bust."

Nikki pulled out a chair opposite Harlan and Kameko and sat down. "A lot of people make that mistake, sir."

"What mistake is that?"

She grinned a little. "Underestimating me."

The director chuckled. "Well, success didn't come without a price."

Her smiled quickly faded. "And what price is that?"

"Have you seen this morning's paper?"

She shook her head.

He leaned over and slid the newspaper across the table toward her. "Page two," he directed.

Nikki unfolded the newspaper and turned to the appropriate page. The headline jumped out at her like a jack-in-the-box: "Harbor Patrol Officer, Mariner Dead after Shootout over Cartel Lieutenant's Vehicle." Underneath the headline was a photograph of the slain officer and the boat pilot. Chills swept up Nikki's spine as she skimmed the rest of the article. "That's not how it went down," she complained.

"What do you mean?" Harlan asked.

Nikki folded the paper closed and laid it back on the table. "Those men were alive when I left the scene."

"And?"

"And they were arguing over the money in the trunk, not the car."

Director Kepler scooped the newspaper up from the table. "What do you suppose happened?"

"Tony Chen, that's what happened." Nikki crossed her arms. "Bastard!"

Director Kepler frowned.

"Street money, when collected, sir," Nikki began, "is always split and placed in two separate duffel bags. When we arrived on the scene, we discovered we were one short. Both the boat pilot and the officer took a keen interest in the lone bag, which was a problem for Chen."

"And your gut feeling on this?"

"If I had to guess, Chen murdered the cop and boat pilot then staged it to look like a fight over a luxury car."

"So this whole shootout—"

"Shoddy journalism at best, but I'm leaning toward blatant media cover-up."

Kameko laughed dryly. "They're pretty much synonymous."

"If Quinn's got a few officers down at the police department on the payroll, how hard is it to buy off an entire newspaper department and get them to print the stories you want printed?" Nikki said, turning toward Harlan.

He gave her a lopsided grin. "A bit conspiratorial, but now that you mention it, entirely plausible." Harlan raised his hand to his chin and cocked his head to one side. "It would be a stroke of genius on his part if he pulled that off, the ultimate in damage control."

"And Lacey?" Nikki asked, changing the subject.

"She's agreed to testify on our behalf."

"In exchange for?"

Harlan's face tightened. "Safekeeping from the Lascano cartel."

"You mean witness protection?"

"Yeess," he replied, drawing out the word.

"It'd better not be Boca Raton or some other country-club setting either," Nikki said.

"It won't be," said Director Kepler. "I can assure you of that. Not on my watch."

Nikki unfolded her arms and relaxed. "I'm thinking some place cold, very cold."

"Fargo, North Dakota," Kameko suggested.

"Nah, the misery index isn't high enough. I'm fond of Adak, Alaska, personally. It's cold, desolate, and remote."

Everyone erupted into laughter. Once it subsided, Kameko excused herself from the group and left the makeshift office. Director Kepler cleared his throat. "Agent Frank?"

"Yes, sir?"

"Since we're all in a festive mood here, I have some additional good news for you."

Nikki leaned forward against the table. "I'm all ears."

"US Attorney Strickland has contacted the state's Violent Offender Assessment committee on your behalf."

"And?" Nikki's hands began to tremble.

"Judge Anderson has waived the packet submission requirement and will allow you to see your brother unrestricted."

Nikki slowly shook her head. "I can't believe this is happening." She gripped her left hand with her right hand in an effort to stop them from shaking. "Finally."

"This," Director Kepler continued, "is a small thank-you from the VOA committee for exposing the corruption festering at the Shaw Women's Correctional Facility."

Nikki loosened the grip on her hands and drew them back down to her side. For a moment, she sat motionless, trying to control her breathing and process everything. Director Kepler moved toward the office door. "There's more."

Nikki's stomach tensed back up. "More?"

"Harlan," he called.

Harlan removed his cell phone from his jacket and activated the direct-connect feature commonly used in dispatch radio systems. "Kameko, stand by. We're en route."

Director Kepler motioned for Nikki to follow him then led

the way out into the warehouse. Once they were out of the office, Harlan took the lead. The trio quickly moved along several primary aisles, past low storage racks and pallets full of freight, and toward the shipping dock.

"Bay seventeen," Harlan announced.

They continued moving forward, single file, until they reached the designated area. Harlan spoke into his cell phone again, and the steel door lifted. Nikki's heart raced as the door inched up. She spotted a pair of silver-and-blue low-cut sneakers. A rush of excitement flooded through her. It was Marty. She knew it instantly, even without the door being fully raised.

Nikki bounced from foot to foot as the door crept higher. A mild tingling sensation churned inside her, causing a smile to pull at her lips. Finally, the door came to a stop. There stood Marty, holding Kameko's hand, at the top of a ground-to-dock-yard ramp.

"Neeka!" he called out, his voice cracking.

Tears welled up in Nikki's eyes. "Right here, Martini."

Marty let go of Kameko's hand and bolted toward his sister. The two embraced. Nikki noticed her brother clutching an envelope. "What's that?" she asked.

Marty smiled then whispered, "For you."

Nikki let go of him and opened the envelope. Inside was a check made out to her for a sizable amount of money. Her jaw dropped. "I've never seen so many zeroes," she said, shaking her head. "At least not in any check made out to me."

Nikki turned to her colleagues for an explanation.

"Back pay," Director Kepler offered. "For three years, six months, and nine days of incarceration, plus accumulated interest."

Nikki's face lit up. "With all the stuff going on, I totally for—"

"There's more," Harlan interrupted. "You're hereby promoted to GS-13, effective immediately."

Nikki clasped her hand to her mouth. For a moment she was speechless.

"The difference in pay," Harlan continued, "has been calculated and is also reflected in the check you're holding. You've sacrificed heavily for this program, and it's time we started taking care of our own."

Nikki was overwhelmed with emotion. She looked around at the faces of her colleagues, smiling as tears flowed down her cheeks. "Thank you, thank you," she said.

Kameko approached her and gave her a warm, extended hug. "Congratulations."

"Thank you, Agent Bolston," Nikki replied.

"Kameko, please."

"Kameko it is." Before Nikki could say anything further, her brother tugged on her shirt. "Yes?" she said, directing her full attention toward him.

Marty pointed at the check in her hand. "What is it, Neeka?"

Nikki smiled. "Assurance that you, Chip, and Wally will continue to live together at Paris Oaks for a very long time."

"Really?"

"Yeah, and that I can visit you as much as I want."

Marty's eyes grew big. "I'd love that."

"Me too, Marty," Nikki replied, hugging him again. "Me too."

NOTE TO READERS

Thank you for reading *Complicity in Heels*.

From speaking with other authors, I know most of them are concerned with getting their work into the hands of as many readers as possible. I'm no different.

There's nothing worse than slaving away on a novel for two to three years, just to have it remain little more than a well-kept secret. What good is it to have written a page-turning story if no one knows about it?

How can you help?

Review this book. It really does matter. When you choose to write a book review, it has the following impact:

It increases the book's ranking on various sites, attracting more potential readers.

It provides feedback to the author about his or her work.

It allows the author to construct better stories in the future.

Again, I'm only asking you to express how you feel about this novel. If you like it, say so, and submit your review. Your opinion matters.

Where can you submit your reviews?

www.amazon.com
www.goodreads.com
www.shelfari.com

Tips

Summarize the storyline without giving away too much of the plot.

Provide your honest reaction. Was the book good, bad, entertaining?

What did you like?

What didn't you like?

Include a favorite scene or line.

Conclude with a recommendation to read or not to read and why.

In closing, I'd like to thank you for your time and for your review. I look forward to better serving you with even more well-constructed stories in the near future.

Sincerely,
Matt Leatherwood Jr.

p.s. A written review opens the door for other readers to follow.

ABOUT THE AUTHOR

Matt Leatherwood Jr. is a former US Marine and a veteran of the Iraq War. Now, instead of leading troops through the desert, he leads readers through well-crafted fiction. *Complicity in Heels* is his debut novel.

Made in the USA
Charleston, SC
02 November 2016